Anne Cameron (Cam Hubert) is well known in Canada
as the author of numerous novels, screenplays, poems and
short stories. Her most famous work is the award-
winning play *Dreamspeaker*. She lives in Nanaimo, British
Columbia.

DAUGHTERS OF COPPER WOMAN

ANNE CAMERON

Published in Great Britain by
The Women's Press Ltd, 1984
A member of the Namara Group
34 Great Sutton Street, London EC1V 0DX

First published in Canada by Press Gang Publishers, 1981

Reprinted 1987, 1990, 1992, 1994

British Library Cataloguing-in-Publication Data
Cameron, Anne
Daughters of Copper Woman
I. Title
813'.54[F]   PR9199.3.C2775

ISBN 0 7043 3946 3

Printed and bound in Great Britain by
Cox & Wyman Ltd, Reading, Berks

For Alex, Erin, Pierre, Marianne, and Kim, with love, and with thanks.

And with gratitude to the Nootka people of the village of Ahousat who share their stories and their lives with me. Special thanks to Margaret Atleo.

In memory of Mary Little.

Preface

For years I have been hearing stories from the native people of Vancouver Island, stories preserved for generations through an oral tradition that is now threatened. Among the stories were special ones shared with me by a few loving women who are members of a secret society whose roots go back beyond recorded history to the dawn of Time itself.

These women shared their stories with me because they knew I would not use them without their permission. Some years ago they gave me permission to write poetry about Old Woman. The summer of 1980 I was told that, if I wanted, I could tell what I knew. The style I have chosen most clearly approaches the style in which the stories were given to me.

A few dedicated women belong to a matriarchal, matrilineal society. These women prefer not to be publicly named or honoured. They prefer that their identity, and the rituals of their society, be kept a secret. I respect their wishes.

Their reasons for sharing their truth, finally, after so many years of protective silence, are explained in the stories. They wish nothing more added to the explanation.

From these few women, with the help of a collective of women, to all other women, with love, and in Sisterhood, this leap of faith that the mistakes and abuse of the past need not continue. There is a better way of doing things. Some of us remember that better way.

Table of Contents

SONG FOR THE DEAD

*The numbers used to introduce the SONG FOR THE DEAD do not
come from the matriarchy. The women who memorized family
lineage and population died in the epidemics. The only surviving
census came from the memorizers of the warrior society; from
their perspective, a man had multiple wives, whereas the women
memorizers' view was that several women shared one husband.*

*The warrior society drew its members from the nobility or
royalty. Commoners and slaves represented the two other levels
of society, and their numbers, like those of the women and
children, were also lost.*

*There were obviously many more people on this island prior
to the coming of the European diseases than the SONG FOR THE
DEAD records. In view of the deaths of the memorizers, the
figures are as accurate a representation as can be made. I believe
thousands more people died and their deaths are unrecorded. I
regret this.*

I N THE 85 years between Captain Cook's visit in 1778
and the Royal Fellowship census in 1863, the Nootka
nation was decimated.

The Nitinat once numbered more than 8000 people; less
than 35 remained.

Yuquot, once home of 2000 men, their multiple wives,
children and slaves, was less than 200.

In Clayoquot Sound more than a thousand warriors, their
multiple wives, children and slaves, had been reduced to a
total of 135.

Tahsis, with more than 2000 fighting men, their multiple
wives, children, and slaves, was shrunk to a total of 60 people.

Civilization brought measles, whooping cough, chicken
pox, diptheria, small pox, tuberculosis, and syphilis.

We are beating the drums
and singing the songs
having a great feast for the dead
for our children are gone
and none remain.
>   *Come back my nephew we miss you*
>   *Come back my daughter we miss you*
>   *Come back my son we miss you*
>   *Come back our lost ones we miss you*
Come back we are lonely
Where have you gone
Come back we are lonely
Where have you gone
>   *Come back we are weeping*
>   *Where have you gone*
>   *Come back we are asking*
>   *Where have you gone*
Come back my brother
Come back my sister
Come back my father
Come back my mother
>   *We will sing a song for you*
>   *We will follow the river to the sea*
>   *And add our tears to the waves*
The tide will rise
The tide will fall
The night will come
The night will go
>   *You will not come*
>   *You who are gone.*

Where did you go?

>   *We are singing our sorrow*
>   *We are singing our grief*
>   *We are singing our farewell*
>   *and our puzzlement*

Why did you go?

OLD MAGIC

*This wind brought another bowl-shaped boat,
and in it three sisters so old and withered
it could not be believed these were women . . .*

THERE WERE NO people on the island, so no human eye saw the oddly shaped craft bob its way up the inlet, propelled only by wind, tide, and the vagaries of the currents. Neither otter nor seal knew nor cared that a gust of wind might smash the hide-bottomed corricle against sheer cliffs; neither cormorant nor eagle knew nor cared that such an event would surely drown the faint spark of life flickering in the emaciated form of the last living person in the bowl-shaped hide boat. The scrawny little form lay still, breathing shallowly, the long hair dull and lank, the lips parted, dry and cracked, in a child's face drawn thin and tight over bones still soft and not yet fully formed.

Old Magic, Old Ways, the Old Ones themselves often seem powerless in a new place. Is it that their force comes from the familiar? Or is it that they allow events to happen, moving only when needed? Or do they have reasons only they can fully understand, reasons for allowing twelve of the original thirteen to leave their shells and pass over within hours of each other, all in the same storm that had brought the corricle to this place? Possibly the twelve had willingly given up their life forces to nourish the spark still flickering in the remaining, precious, youngest, thirteenth child whose green eyes were hidden by the thin pale lids, the tawny lashes not even fluttering, so great was her exhaustion.

On a coast dominated by rock and cliff, where mountains spring from the sea and rivers run unchecked through deep-cut channels, on a coast where even in warm weather the ocean is cold and human life cannot long survive, where the water is unfathomably deep, on a coast bathed in the beauty of a harsh and stark reality, the frail craft came to rest on a rare and miraculous thing, a beach. A beach protected by rocks and reefs, and how the small hide shell missed annihilation, only the Old Ones can say.

The tide was at its fullest, an autumn high tide, the water washing the beach several feet past the normal tidal mark, and when the pull of the moon changed and the water receded, the small craft was left on hardpacked gravel. A beach, but not a sandy beach; rocks, round small rocks of every colour, tone, and shade, and when the brief rain squall dropped its damp burden, the cool drops fell on parched, cracked lips, half open with weakness, and it was only automatic reflex that caused the swollen, blackened tongue to lick feebly. The rain gathered in the bottom of the small craft, soaking the few meagre rags remaining on the wasted body of the little girl. Her long hair, straggling across her face, collected the water so it ran into her mouth. Her dehydrated body absorbed the water, her salt-poisoned skin was washed clean and the small hard stones began to poke through the veil of misery and unconsciousness until she stirred, moaning protest. The change in position, the shifting of weight, sent the small craft onto its side and the emaciated little girl rolled out, landing in a small freshwater drainage cut. She half opened her eyes, and like an animal, instinctively licked the water, sucking noisily, letting the last of the salt and dirt run from her, back into the earth.

The rain squall passed and for many long moments the child lay, slowly sipping and lapping water. Twice her stomach rebelled and she heaved, turning her head aside so as not to spew into the creek, and soon she was able to sit up, look around her with red-rimmed and swollen eyes.

She struggled to her feet and pulled herself upright. Not far from her a large boulder stuck up out of the receding sea, and on it, clusters of blue-shelled mussels, far bigger than the ones she had known in her own place, but familiar enough to her that she moved painfully to the rock and began to pick them off, cracking them open and sucking the flesh raw from the cradle-like half shells. Her stomach was so shrunken it only took a few and she was satisfied. Another drink of water, and she lay down on the ground beneath a large hemlock tree, and cuddled close to the living trunk. She slept on moss and mulch still dry in spite of the storms, the rain shed by the overhang of evergreen. When she wakened, she ate more mussels, drank more of the fresh water, and then slept again, her body gaining strength. When she stirred next it was night, and the stars overhead were visible for the first time since the sudden and unexpected high wind had boiled up out of the sea. She searched the heaven, studying the shapes and placement of the patterns written in the night, and soon she knew she was here. She didn't know where Here was.

From the small boat came the faint but unmistakable scent of first decomposition, and she wept openly when she looked down on the wretched and contorted forms of the sisters. Twelve of the chosen ones, twelve of the high degree, dead of thirst, for the water they needed they had given to her, each one claiming every time that yes, she had indeed sipped her share. Dead of cold, for what few scraps of cloth remained from their robes had been placed over the child, protecting her from the biting teeth of the wind. Dead of hunger, for as with the water, each had claimed to have nibbled her portion of the pitifully inadequate stock of food and urged the child to eat. Twelve of the chosen sisters voluntarily preparing to pass over so that the child, and the knowledge she bore, could survive and continue.

Painfully she pulled the small boat closer to shore, stopping several times to eat of the mussels, knowing not to gorge herself, resting when the waves of dizziness hit her, weeping when her sorrow become too large for her to swallow, until she was strong enough to do for them the needed thing, the last thing she could do for those who had done so much for her.

All around the beach pieces of wood lay scattered, left behind by the coming and going of the tides, bleached and made dry by the hot summer sun, and only the outside of them dampened by the rain squall. From them a pleasant smell, not of oak, nor even of the tough evergreen trees that grew to the north of her former home, but a cheerful and encouraging smell. All around her, tall trees, noble, straight, thrusting toward heaven, and green, from bottom to top, sacred green. Heartened, she dragged the wood, piece by piece, bit by bit, to a seemly place and began to do that which must be done. Before long, she was again tired, and returned to her place under the protective tree. When she awakened, the sun was coming from her night resting place, and already the morning mist was burning away, and with another meal of mussels and more of the fresh water, she returned to her task. As the sun was ready to hide her head behind a mountain, the girl child was ready. The pyre stood tall, as tall as she could make it, and inside the pyre were the bodies of the sisters, so swollen now, and so changed, she could not easily recognize them. Those who pass over together of their own will should be sent off together, and so in the pyre, four tiers, three sisters to a tier, magic four, as the four winds, the four directions, the four parts of a tree, the four seasons. From the corricle she took the small box and moved to the pyre, saying the words, choking sometimes on sobs. From the trees she took hanging dry moss and though they were not the trees of the old ways, still they supplied the means to do that which must be done, so that even in the new was that which was needed to fulfill the Old.

The barbarians had come from the cold places, and though the priests and poets, the simple and lordly, all had rallied, the Old Ones did not waken, nor had they moved to use the Power against the bearded giants. Time and again the magic did not do what was needed, and so the council gathered and told them all that, when this happened, it did not mean the magic was gone, nor did it mean the Old Ones were angry, it meant simply that it was Time. Time for movement, Time for change, Time for expansion, Time to do as do the trees in their time, move the seeds on the wings of the wind. And so the small boats set out from the places, and in each boat a coming-together group, trusting their lives to small craft made of hides stretched over frail wood, trusting to the winds and the currents, moving with Time and with Change, boat losing contact with other boats until, for the girl and her matrix sisters there had been only the endless waves and a sea that offered little, for they did not know how to fish these deep waters, and slowly, sacrificially, life and force ebbed from them to protect her.

The flint struck sparks into the moss and as the glow spread to become flame she chanted the old words and made rune signs in the sand. The new wood did not burn as cleanly as the old, it sent torrents of sparks racing to the sky, made happy, crackling noises, and seemed to celebrate.

And why not? To be the first wood in a new land to be so honoured as to take the chosen home? Not only one chosen, but twelve, going to the Old Ones, going to fulfill their Time.

All night long the pyre burned, and four times she added fresh logs from those she had piled nearby. She sang and wept, made rune signs and sobbed, for though those warmed by the flames no longer had any worries, she knew she would be lonely.

She fell asleep by the pyre and when she wakened, the fire was low, the sun was high. She prayed, then resolutely turned from the pyre and drank of the cold fresh water. Then she went looking for food.

Oysters she placed near the pyre and the heat simmered them until the shells opened and the meat was hers for the taking. Large, some twice as big as her hand, and what she could not eat she put into the pyre flames as thanks offering. Something in the wind told her the cold would soon take this land, something in the angle of the sun and stars told her she had missed the best weather, and in the days and nights following, she prepared to pit the old knowledge against the new threats.

She searched doggedly until she found a proper large hole in the rock mountain, and then to it she took the familiar things left to her by her passed over sisters. The rune cast sticks, the herb stores, the sacred rocks and the knife used to blunt and cut pain during birth. With hide from the boat she painstakingly fashioned a cover for the entrance hole to keep out the wind that blew more bitterly every day. Wood she salvaged and piled under trees where it would stay reasonably dry and at least not be washed out with the tides. And from the stars she knew no foreign invader would come here, not this Time, no triumph would gleam in pagan eyes as he forced his flesh into the body of a believer. She was safe, and the old magic, what she knew of it, was safe; if it was diminished by the absence of the other twelve, still, this had happened before, and each time, when it was Time, that which was needed had been found, that which had been forgotten had been re-learned. Or given. To Endure was all that was required of her.

And she endured. Endured. She learned to weave weirs to lay out at high tide and when the water went down at low tide, caught in the weirs were fish to be speared or netted, or sometimes grabbed with bare hands.

She Endured. And survived. Marginally, perhaps, but it is not required of us that we live well. Throughout the long wet winter, even when the snow lay deep on the mountain and ice blocked the rivulets, she Endured. Throughout the following spring and summer, drying berries and finding the nests of birds, scavenging and surviving, she Endured. Only an idiot could have starved on the coast and none of the daughters had ever been idiots.

She Endured. Her child body ripened, her fair skin darkened with the sun and wind, and, with a full moon in the middle of her fourth winter of rain and bitter wind, loneliness and endurance, came proof she was a woman. Then, and with each moon cycle, she was reminded that there had been no ritual, no passing on of further adult knowledge, no public demonstration of pride. She wondered if this meant that with the Time of Change had come a loss of this woman pride. At first it did not bother her that there had been no ceremony, with the young priests all offering themselves for her if she so wished, but as the months became years, she wondered what it would have been like for her if it had not been a Time of Change.

It was the wind that brought them. The wind of autumn that blows for days down the inlet, bringing no rain, but in it trapped the voices of the screaming lost souls, howling and weeping, pulling at the trees, wearing at the rocks. Even when the sun is bright and the air warm with the last of summer, the wind wails for the dying of another season.

This wind brought another bowl-shaped boat, and in it three sisters so old and withered it could not be believed these were women. They had heard from the Old Ones that there was a chosen young sister, a sister in need, and had come to give her that which they alone could give, and then only willingly, the secrets locked inside their heads.

She nursed them, kept them warm, and fed them, and all the loneliness of all the years burst forth in a flame of love so bright it kept the old woman alive long after that time when they should have passed over, and they talked to her, teaching the secrets and mysteries at a rate that broke all tradition. What should have taken half a lifetime was pushed on her in a few months, without ceremony or ritual, and she, so starved for human voice, absorbed every word.

The cold winter took the first old sister; she had emptied her shell of all wisdom and teaching, and only love kept her dry husk alive, until she asked the young copper-skinned woman to allow her to leave her meat and bones behind and go to the Old Ones. And the young woman wept, and built the pyre, and with the two remaining old sisters made the runes and said the words and sent the frail shell off in a shower of sparks, and even the winter wind was shamed and stopped its screaming so the smoke and sparks went straight to the night sky.

The young woman told the two remaining sisters of her fears and loneliness, and from them she learned all sisters enter the wasteland. For some the form is different than for others, but the wasteland is always what it is. Some never pass through, and these ones never learn the truths; some pass part way through and being only part way through are lost and forget what they have learned. A chosen number, by their own efforts and determination, come through the wasteland, and to them are given the secrets, and it was because the young woman had Endured as well as she had that the old women came in search of her.

She learned she had been Known at birth, for her eyes bespoke her destiny, green as the sea, the sign of the Special, green as the trees, the grass, and the leaves, and when she pointed out not all the sisters had green eyes the old women laughed the dry grass-rustling laugh and told her many are born, few are chosen, and even fewer are Special, and the green eyes are the sign of an old soul re-born. Only the Special are chosen at birth, the others are found when it is Time, found by attitude and skill, sometimes even by accident.

And then the blue-eyed sister passed over and was sent off with the sparks and the runes, the prayers and the tears, and the copper-skinned young woman with the green eyes began to weep bitterly, for she knew the last surviving sister had but precious hours to live, and then she would again be alone. Alone with a body ripe for bearing but fruitless, alone with only sea, mountains, trees and herSelf.

The old woman watched for long moments, then, in a great outpouring of love, even as her life flickered haltingly, she rallied, and gave the copper woman the greatest secret of all, delaying even her own passing-over to share the final secret, and perhaps that is why as the old woman passed over

20

part of her spirit stayed in the body of the young copper woman, reborn and revitalized in the body of the chosen one.

For a fourth time a pyre was built and the runes written. For a fourth time the words were said and the smoke rose to heaven. With the completion of the magic four, the place became forever sacred, never again to be just an ordinary beach, but always and forever a gathering place for spirits and those gone beyond our ken. Those who are familiar with the truth of the Time, even though no one will ever tell which bay or cove or beach is The One, know when they have arrived at The Place, know it by the feelings and the textures, by the communication of spirits, and always with the Knowing comes the confidence that at some time, some Time, a previous body made a previous visit, for this is the continuity of spirit sharing.

COPPER WOMAN

Copper Woman did as she was told.
Not understanding, but having faith,
she scooped the mess up in a mussel shell
and put it with her magic things.
A few days later she noticed that
the sand in the shell was moving . . .

I N THE DAYS before the coming of the people, the coast was
almost empty. Only Copper Woman lived here, alone
with her secrets, her mysteries and herSelf. Copper
Woman lived, but not well, for her secrets were incomplete
and her cycle unfinished, her world not yet a totality.

Alone she came from the bowels of the mountains and
built on the shoreline a small wooden house. Alone she learned to harvest Tutsup the sea urchin, Ya-is the butter clam,
Hetchen the little neck clam, Ah-sam the crab, Um-echt the
horse clam, and So-ha the spring salmon. She learned to eat
the meat and make clothes from Kich-tlatz the fur seal. Alone
she learned Tut-lukh the sea lion was not to be approached
unwarily. But still, her existence was marginal at best.

In the time of the first autumn storms a craft of godling
creatures appeared and taught Copper Woman all she must
know to survive on a better level. Coming from the setting
sun, riding down the golden slide that cuts across the water
just before the blanket of nightfall, they came to teach her
what all humankind must Know to live more fully. But this

was not the Time nor the Place for the magic ones to stay, and as they left for their place, Copper Woman began to weep. Bitterly she cried, for loneliness is a bitter thing and an acrid taste in our mouths, more bitter when you think you have been freed from it and find it returning again. So much did she cry, her very head began to drain of all fluid and as tears fell from her eyes, from her nose fell great amounts of thick mucus. Tears and mucus and from her mouth saliva, and her face swelled as the waters of loneliness poured. From her nose an enormous cluster of mucus strands fell onto the sand and lay at her feet, and so great was the cluster that even in her pathetic state, Copper Woman was aware of it and grew ashamed. Trying to conquer her wailing, she tried to kick sand over the mess, bury it, hide it, return it to the earth. The magic women told her not to feel shame, not to bury the snot, but to save it, even cherish it, and when she had learned to accept even this most gross evidence of her own mortality, then from the acceptance would come the means whereby she would never again be alone, never again be lonely. They told her that those times when body secretions flow, those times when a woman answers the call of the moon, are holy and sacred times, times for prayer and contemplation.

Copper Woman did as she was told. Not understanding, but having faith, she scooped the mess up in a mussel shell and put it with her magic things. A few days later she noticed that the sand in the shell was moving. She looked closely and saw a small, incomplete thing twisting uncomfortably in the small shell. Copper Woman carefully placed what was in the mussel shell in a larger shell, a shell of Um-echt the horse clam. Every day she watched and become aware that the small living incomplete thing was growing something that looked like a miniature of the neck of the horse clam. Soon the small figure was too large to be comfortable in the shell of Um-echt, so she put it in a shell of Tutsup the sea urchin. But in only a day or two she moved it again, for beneath the thing that looked like the neck of Un-echt, this thing was developing small versions of Tutsup, and

Copper Woman did not want the spines of the sea urchin to grow between the legs of her little friend, for then how would he walk? So she put him in the shell of Ah-sam the crab and for a few weeks he was happy, although, like Ah-Sam, he would grab at her with his hands and not want to let go. Copper Woman put her little mannikin in a bed made of fur from Tut-lukh the sea lion and he was happy enough, even though on his face he grew whiskers like Tut-lukh and on parts of his chest and belly the soft fur of the big animal. And his voice became deep and he would roar with jealousy if Copper Woman spent too much time admiring something else.

One night the snot boy left his bed of fur from Tut-lukh and crawled in bed with Copper Woman. He fastened his mouth, like the mouth of Ah-Sam, on her mouth, and his hands, grasping like the claws of Ah-Sam, felt for her breasts. Copper Woman knew she could easily destroy this impertinent snot boy, but she also felt responsible for him and sorry for him for being such an incomplete collection of traits from a number of sea creatures. Had not the sea saved her? Had not the god women come from the sea and told her this strange thing would be the means whereby she would never again be alone? Besides, his mouth on hers was pleasant, and his hands, though demanding, were not hurtful and caused a warmth in her belly. A warmth that grew until the part of him made from the neck of Um-echt and the parts of him which resembled Tutsup began to come alive and grow and she welcomed Um-echt into her body and held the snot boy close to her, closer, until the lonely feeling almost — but not quite — went away, and she felt her body swelling, filling as if with the moon.

The snot boy cried out, not the deep voice of Tut-lukh but a cry much like that of Qui-na the gull, and then the mannikin held onto her and shook as if the autumn gales were within him. Copper Woman soothed him and held him close and wondered if the loneliness would ever totally go. Many times thereafter she would hold the snot boy close and fix her mouth on his, use the magic of her hands to waken the two small Tutsup and once they were awake the Um-echt part entered her, seeking, exploring, taking her — almost — from loneliness, but never totally.

MOWITA

. . . and Copper Woman looked at her daughter
and felt the loneliness diminish until
it was no larger than a small round pebble
on the beach . . .

COPPER WOMAN WAS living with Snot Boy, the incomplete mannikin, in the place where the god women had come to give her knowledge. She taught the small strange creature as much as she could, but he never really seemed to learn properly. When he built a weir, there was always one part of it not properly made, and many of the fish would escape. When he built a fire it was either too hot or not hot enough, and often he would burn himself. When he was through using a thing, he would leave it, never remembering to put it away where he could find it again, and sometimes he would forget to come home when the meal was ready, then would complain bitterly if his food was overdone or cold. Copper Woman would tease him, make him forget his ill humour, laugh with him and often she would sing for him, for she was less lonely with him than she had been when alone.

Her breasts grew large and tender, her belly filled until it looked as if the moon itself was trapped inside, and one day movement within her told her she was no longer one person, but two, that there was another living inside her body. Copper Woman prayed daily that this other would not be incomplete like the Snot Boy, but rather an entire person, capable of responsibility and attention to detail. Often she felt frightened and wondered at her own ability to care for this new person, and once or twice she chafed to think she was no longer free to be herself, but had to think in terms of another.

One night, with much pain and blood, there came from her a small version of herself. But altered. The copper skin was darker, and the hair black, even blacker than that of Ku-ka-was the hair seal. The eyes were more slanted than hers, almost like those of the cormorant, who had no other name yet and only got their name much later when the blindness was taken from them. And Copper Woman looked at her daughter and felt the loneliness diminish until it was no larger than a small round pebble on the beach. Her breasts ached with a pulsation like that of the waves on the beach and when she had cleaned the blood from her daughter and the mucus from the small nose and mouth, she wept with thanks for the secret magic the Old Ones had given her. Knowing the secret she had been able to lick clean her child and not feel revulsion. Rather, she felt that again, but in a different way, she was giving life to herSelf. When she held her child close, to warm her and make her welcome, the small head turned and the soft mouth closed around the swollen and darkened nipple. The small pebble of loneliness vanished and a feeling even stronger than those awakened by Snot Boy filled Copper Woman until it was as if the magic women themselves had entered into her, through her to her milk, and from the milk to the child, so she named the child Mowita, knowing she would one day be a matriarch.

Snot Boy did not pay much attention to Mowita. Sometimes he would play with her, sometimes he would even hold her and speak softly to her, but mostly he went about his own affairs. Incomplete, he could catch fish, but it was Copper Woman, and later, Mowita, who knew how to smoke and cure. Time and again they showed Snot Boy how to do it, but he would laugh and say he had no time for such bothersome details, and he would leave, laughing. He could catch Mowitch the deer, but was useless curing the hide or cooking the meat.

When Mowita was walking and laughing and beginning to make words, Copper Woman gave life to a son, like Snot Boy, but not quite so incomplete. Not as complete as Mowita, but more so than Snot Boy. And when this child was walking there was another, again a girl, and to her daughters Copper Woman taught the secrets, to her sons she tried to teach more than Snot Boy would ever know. Many children had Copper Woman, and their laughter rang clearly, riding on the wind, climbing to the heavens as does the smoke of a fire, and life for them was pleasant.

QOLUS THE CHANGEABLE

*One day Qolos told Thunderbird she wanted
to live on earth, for it seemed there was more
to do than sit or fly. Thunderbird said the
decision was hers to make but she must remember
that when one changes form
one changes totally . . .*

THERE ARE FOUR kingdoms to reality. The kingdom of earth, that of the underground, that under the sea, and that of the heavens.

The kingdom of the heavens was ruled by Thunderbird. When he opened his eyes the sun shone, when he ruffled his feathers the wind blew, when he waved his great wings the colours would flash and we would call it lightning, and when he slapped his wings together came the noise we call thunder. Thunderbird ruled with his wife Qolus. Like Thunderbird she was made of bright feathers, although she had no horns on her head, and she had little to do but fly around the heavens with Thunderbird keeping the clouds in their places, sending rain when it was needed, and waiting. Waiting. Waiting.

Qolus spent much time watching Copper Woman and her children. Especially Mowita, the oldest, the first born, the most special of gifts. Mowita was growing now to womanhood but was still a girl, and her graceful movements and happy laughter warmed Qolus and made her happy. One day Qolus told Thunderbird she wanted to live on earth, for it seemed there was more to do than sit or fly. Thunderbird said the decision was hers to make but she must remember that when one changes form one changes totally. Qolus still wanted to leave the kingdom of the heavens and go to earth. So she changed form. So completely did she change she arrived on earth as Mah Teg Yelah, the first man. Snot Boy, the incomplete, would never be a man and the sons of Copper Woman were still little boys, and not as many lived as had been born for some had died from fighting or recklessness.

Mah Teg Yelah looked on the daughters of earth and considered them fair. He set to building a house larger than any on earth for he wished to impress the daughters of Copper Woman. But when the house was half built he found the ridge pole too heavy to lift into place so called on Thunderbird to help. Coming to earth, his magic feathers flashing, Thunderbird first changed himself into human form so he could talk and when he understood the problem he changed back to himself and in his mighty talons took the lodgepole and lifted it in place. Copper Woman and her daughters were watching and saw all this and knew Mah Teg Yelah was magical and Copper Woman was pleased. When the house was built and Mah Teg Yelah asked Mowita to be his wife, Copper Woman did not disagree. Mowita, herself, was not interested in having to spend her life caring for an incomplete one like Snot Boy or her brothers, and so she agreed and became the wife of Mah Teg Yelah who had been Qolus the changeable, wife of Thunderbird. They had four sons and the sons, all magical like their mother and father, grew well and quickly.

Time to those in the heavens is not as Time to those on earth and Mah Teg Yelah pined for the skies for it seemed to take forever to do anything on earth. Still, he had his wife and children to care for so he stayed.

Thunderbird himself was lonely, though Time for him passed more quickly, and so it was that the sons were nearly men before the loneliness began to affect Thunderbird, for he missed Qolus and knew she was not totally happy as Mah Teg Yelah.

Thunderbird began to weep. He did not intend to cause any harm to anybody, but he was lonely and his Qolus was not happy, and so Thunderbird wept. Copper Woman told Mowita the rain would not stop until each finger on either hand had seen four, magic four, days of rain.

Mowita set to work with Mah Teg Yelah and covered the entire log house with pitch. Her brothers laughed at her. Her sisters helped her. And as the water rose and the house began to float, the sisters of Mowita entered the waterproof house, too. Copper Woman said she did not have to go into the house, which was getting very crowded, she would be safe with her magic. It was Time, she said, for her skin to split anyway, Time for her to allow her children to go off on their own and not stay tied to her forever. So she left her bag of meat and bones on the beach and went to visit with her magical sisters.

For days the house floated, then Mah Teg Yelah sent Raven out to see if the land was still there. Raven returned wet, and tired, and said there was no place to even rest, everything was water. Some days later Mah Teg Yelah sent the Raven out again and this time she brought back the promise of life, a sprig of cedar. Still the water covered all but the tops of the tallest trees and there was no place for Raven to rest. A few days later Raven was again sent out and this time she came to a window, dropped a sprig of hemlock, then flew away again. When Raven flew away all inside the house knew it was safe outside and so they opened the pitch-sealed door and indeed, there were again mountains, valleys, rivers, lakes, and grassy ground beneath their feet. And from that time on hemlock has been used as protection against drowning.

The animals in the pitch-sealed house ran happily outside, then the daughters of Copper Woman prepared to leave. But the sons of Mowita and Mah Teg Yelah said they wished to go with the women, and so they did, four couples going off in four different directions, and from them came all the people of the world. One couple became the parents of the black people, one couple became the parents of the yellow people, one couple became the parents of the white people, and one couple became the parents of the Indian people, and so we are all related, for we all come from the Belly of Copper Woman.

Mowita looked at Mah Teg Yelah as their sons left with her sisters to populate the earth, and she knew he yearned for the heavens. She told him it was Time, his duties as a father were finished, his duties as husband were fulfilled, and he was happy. Calling on Thunderbird, he changed back into Qolus, and Mowita watched Qolus fly upward to join her husband.

Then Mowita sat and wondered if now she, too, would be alone. She wept to not have her sons, her sisters, her husband, her mother. After she had wept, she rose, and set about the task of re-establishing a life for herself, and for many days and weeks she did the things that needed to be done, the day-to-day things that must be done to sustain life. She set weirs, she cleaned and smoked fish, she mended clothes, gathered wood for her fire, kept her freshwater spring clean and grew to accept and even cherish solitude. And one day, busying herself at her work and knowing a contentment because she had learned she could endure and survive by herself, Mowita looked up and from the forest came Copper Woman, her mother, back in new skin, back from her visit to her magical sisters, back from that source place across the path the sun makes, when it sinks behind the water for its rest. And a gladness stirred in Mowita, for she was not alone, and she ran to her mother and embraced her and they laughed and wept with joy. Some months later the gladness came forth and was twin girls, one with green eyes like her grandmother, and thereafter, every so many years, Mowita would carry happiness inside herself and the Children of Happiness grew strong and their laughter echoed, and there was much music in their lives. The Children of Happiness had children of their own and Copper Woman grew old, spending her time with her grandchildren, teaching the girls the secrets of women, and this time even some of the boys could learn, for they were more complete than the sons of the incomplete Snot Boy, for Qolus/Mah Teg Yelah had proven, having been in his own time and place a wife, that in every woman dwell aspects of man, and in every man aspects of woman, so there is never any need for conflict.

Copper Woman knew her flesh was failing, interfering with her abilities, so she turned much of the responsibility over to Mowita. When Copper Woman was so old even she could not remember how old, she became Old Woman. When Old Woman was so bent with age she could sweep the beach clean without having to reach down, she told Mowita it was again Time. Old Woman Knew, and it was Time.

Her skin split, she again left her meat and bones on the beach, and she came from within, her Self freed. Mowita wept to know her mother was gone, and she wondered if she could survive and endure, and be and do all that Old Woman had been and done. She heard the daughter with the green eyes chanting the words to Old Woman, asking Old Woman to enter her, become her. Then the daughter with the green eyes, whose name is known only to the initiates, lay down on a bed of skins, and Old Woman, hidden in the skins, became pregnant. From this the green-eyed daughter lived as part of Old Woman, and lived in Old Woman, who was also part of and in her. And there is no easy answer to the questions and puzzlement that comes with being told this, the answer lies within each of us, and we must each find that answer for ourselves. And Mowita knew, then, it was not necessary for her to do all and be all that Old Woman had been and done, for the secrets were shared, and Old Woman was not Gone, only Changed, and would answer when needed. Mowita also knew that when it came close to her Time there would be another to take her place, and when it came close to the Time of the green-eyed daughter, one would be recognized to replace her, and if it was not known before the Time to pass over, it would be known after. But always the truth will be sustained and the secrets will Endure, for Old Woman is watching, Old Woman is guarding, and with her all things are possible. When Mowita was Old Woman, she told the green-eyed daughter to prepare the rituals and be ready to continue as, and allow to come out of her, that part of Old Woman which was in her. And always the disciples will aid the Old Woman and give her strength, the initiates will aid the disciples and the women will protect their Truth, glory in it and Endure.

And though all of this happened so long ago nobody can say when, still there are women who Know, and whether they are women who come from the lines of the four couples, or whether they are of the line of happiness, still they may Know. And still, many are born but few are chosen. And still those who come with green eyes are held in esteem. Some are born, some come in search, and if they Know they are welcomed, so that within the Women's Society neither wealth nor social position count, for these are imposed on earth by chance and whim, while within the society only that which grows from the core has any meaning.

When the Time came for the next change and the black robed men moved to destroy the Society of Women, the women Endured. Not fighting, not disputing, clinging to their knowledge, they Endured, and now it is almost Time again, and much magic is preparing, and soon the sign will be known.

SISIUTL

There are some people that think that only people
have emotions like pride, fear, and joy,
but those who know will tell you
all things are alive . . .

THERE ARE TREES on the coast stripped of bark, stark
silver white, and without the bark one can see how
the very wood is twisted so the dead tree seems to be
like a corkscrew rooted in the earth. There are people who
think that only people have emotions like pride, fear, and joy,
but those who know will tell you all things are alive, perhaps
not in the same way we are alive, but each in its own way,
as should be, for we are not all the same. And though different from us in shape and life span, different in Time and
Knowing, yet are trees alive. And rocks. And water. And all
know emotion.

There are rocks on the coast which, like the trees, seem
corkscrewed, seem to twist upon themselves, as if in agony.
Whirlpools and riptides are the same, only different. All
because they have seen Sisiutl and tried to flee.

Sisiutl, the fearsome monster of the sea. Sisiutl who sees
from front and back. Sisiutl the soul searcher. Sisiutl whose
familiars are often known as Stlalacum, the vision people,

those who ride on the wind and bring dreams, the Stlalacum who search out the chosen and those who would see beyond the externals.

Sisiutl moves freely in water whether salt or fresh, even in heavy rain, for he is able to transform himself. He seeks those who cannot control their fear, who do not have a Truth.

Fearful he is and terrifying. His eyes send cold fire into your belly and his forked serpent tongue flashes horror at your soul. No words could explain Sisiutl, who looks like a snake, but has no tail, rather a head at both ends, each head more fearsome than the other, and from him emanates cold and horror.

When you see Sisiutl you must stand and face him. Face the horror. Face the fear. If you break faith with what you Know, if you try to flee, Sisiutl will blow with both mouths at once and you will begin to spin. Not rooted in the earth as are the trees and rocks, not eternal as are the tides and currents, your corkscrew spinning will cause you to leave the earth, to wander forever, a lost soul, and your voice will be heard in the screaming winds of first autumn, sobbing, pleading, begging for release. Lost, no part of the Stlalacum who know Truth, no part of anything, alone, and lonely, and lost forever.

The bark flew from the frightened trees leaving only the twisted wood exposed. Only the roots, deep in the earth, kept the trees from falling upward into the void.

When you see Sisiutl the terrifying, though you be frightened, stand firm. There is no shame in being frightened, only a fool would not be afraid of Sisiutl the horror. Stand firm, and if you know protective words, say them. First one head, then the other, will rise from the water. Closer. Closer. Coming for your face, the ugly heads, closer, and the stench from the devouring mouths, and the cold, and the terror. Stand firm. Before the twin mouths of Sisiutl can fasten on your face and steal your soul, each head must turn towards you. When this happens, Sisiutl will see his own face.

Who sees the other half of Self, sees Truth.

36

Sisiutl spends eternity in search of Truth. In search of those who know Truth. When he sees his own face, his own other face, when he looks into his own eyes, he has found Truth.

He will bless you with magic, he will go, and your Truth will be yours forever. Though at times it may be tested, even weakened, the magic of Sisiutl, his blessing, is that your Truth will endure.

And the sweet Stlalacum will visit you often, reminding you your Truth will be found behind your own eyes.

And you will not be Alone again.

THE CHILDREN OF HAPPINESS

*Children of Happiness are not like
ordinary children . . .*

MOWITA WAS LIVING alone in the place where the cedar-pitched waterproof house had been deposited when the flood receded, and she was very lonely. She was used to the company of her husband Mah Teg Yelah, and the laughter of her sons and their wives, her sisters. She was used to having long talks with her mother, Copper Woman, and with her sisters who were also her daughters-in-law, but she was alone.

The four couples had gone to repopulate the world, and Mah Teg Yelah had become Qolus again, and returned to the heavens and to the song of the wind in her strong wing feathers. Mowita spent her days collecting food; more than she would ever need. She kept her house clean, and made clothes she felt she would never need to wear. And she wondered what she had done to be left so alone.

She wondered why it was that, when the four couples left to repopulate the world and Mah Teg Yelah again became

Qolus, Copper Woman had decided to travel the path the sun makes across the water when it sets for the night, and had gone away in her dugout and left Mowita alone. Alone for such a long time that she could barely remember what it was like not to be alone.

She sang all the songs she knew, she danced all the dances she knew, she remembered all she had been taught, and she looked into herself for answers. And one day she looked up, and there was her mother walking toward her, holding out her hands and smiling.

Mowita looked at her mother and was filled with happiness of such magnitude she thought she would split open and her spirit fly free on the wind. She ran to her mother, and embraced her, and kissed her, and cried with joy. That night the small cedar-pitched waterproof house was bright with light and laughter and ripe with the voices of two women. And the happiness grew in Mowita until she could feel it moving under her heart.

Some months later the happiness was born and came into the world as twin baby girls, one with green eyes like her grandmother. And her name is so sacred only a few are allowed to know it. She and her sister were the first of the Children of Happiness.

Children of Happiness are not like ordinary children. They are usually little girls, but sometimes little boys are born with the signs. You can tell one of the Children of Happiness by the way it is different. A Child of Happiness always seems like an old soul living in a new body, and her face is very serious until she smiles, and then the sun lights up the world. You look at the eyes of a Child of Happiness and you Know the child knows everything that is truly important. Children of Happiness always look not quite the same as other children. They have strong, straight legs and walk with purpose. They laugh as do all children, and they play as do all children, they talk child talk as do all children, but they are different, they are blessed, they are special, they are sacred.

THE CHILDREN OF HAPPINESS

They are to be cherished and protected,
even at the risk of your life.
They will know sadness, but will overcome it.
They will know alienation
for they see past and through this reality.
They will Endure where others cannot.
They will Survive where others cannot.
They know love even when it is not shown to them.

They spend their lives trying to Communicate
the love they know.

OLD WOMAN

*And Copper Woman was tired. She felt there were
other things for her to do,
things she could not do in human form . . .*

COPPER WOMAN HAD been alive for many generations
but had not changed. Her body was still strong and
lithe, her skin had darkened to a rich brown in the
sunlight, but her hair was still the colour of copper, and her
eyes were still the green of the sea on a calm day, and her
skin had only a few lines around the eyes and some lines
around the mouth where she smiled often.

But she had been alive for many years. Her granddaughters were grandmothers now, and the children of the
four sons of Mowita and the four daughters of Copper
Woman were many, and their children even more numerous.
And Copper Woman was tired. She felt there were other
things for her to do, things she could not do in human form,
things she wanted to see that she could not see in her dugout,
and so she talked to Mowita, her firstborn, and told her
what she was thinking.

41

Mowita wept, but she knew the Time had come full. And she called for her daughter Hai Nai Yu, whose name means The Wise One or The One Who Knows, or several other things, and talked to her, and Hai Nai Yu listened, and went with her grandmother to the waiting house, and they sat on the moss and let the blood of the woman's time flow back to the earth and Copper Woman told Hai Nai Yu things she had not even told Mowita. Hai Nai Yu listened, and learned, and the wisdom was safe.

Then Copper Woman told Hai Nai Yu that the wisdom must always be passed on to women, and reminded her that whatever the colour of the skin, all people come from the same blood and the blood is sacred. She said a time would come when the wisdom would nearly disappear, but it would never perish, and whenever it was needed, a way would be found to present it to the women, and they could then decide if they wanted to learn it or not. And Hai Nai Yu promised that when it came Time for her, she would be sure there was someone to replace her as the guardian of the wisdom.

Copper Woman warned Hai Nai Yu that the world would change and times might come when Knowing would not be the same as Doing. And she told her that Trying would always be very important.

Then she left the waiting house for the last time, and she ate a last meal with her family. She held them all, and kissed them all, and reassured them she would always be there if there was Need.

Then she walked to the beach and sat by herself and waited until the sun was gone and the moon was high in the sky, painting the waves with silver. She stood then, and said the words, sang the songs, danced the dances and prayed the prayers.

Then she left her meat in her bag of skin, and took her bones with her, and became a spirit. She became Old Woman. She turned her bones into a broom and a loom.

OLD WOMAN

With the loom she weaves the pattern of destiny.
With her broom she sweeps clean the beach
and the minds of all women who call on her

She became part of fog mist and night wind
she became part of sea spray and waves
she became part of rain and storm
she became part of sunshine and clear sky.

She became part of night and part of day
she became part of winter and part of summer
she became part of spring and part of fall
she became part of all of creation.

With her loom and with her broom
with her love and with her patience
she weaves the pattern of destiny
and sweeps beaches and minds
she weaves the pattern of reality
and tidies shorelines and souls.

She will never abandon you.

TEM EYOS KI

She sang of a place so wondrous the minds
of people could not even begin to imagine it . . .

MANY GENERATIONS AFTER Old Woman freed herself
from her meat and bag of skin, many years after
the secrets began to be taught by and to the chosen
women, the first period of testing occurred, a period Old
Woman had known would occur.

The women for centuries had not concerned themselves
with politics or argument. They left these things to the men,
to give them something to occupy themselves with during the
long dark months of winter. The women concerned
themselves with spiritual things and with studying the
teachings of the society, and with children, and keeping the
society strong, and with making sure life was lived as it
ought to be, fully, and with contentment.

The women became complacent. They thought because
things had Always been so, they would Always remain so.
And they did not notice that the men had begun to dominate
many areas of society. Had become powerful. Had begun to
believe their power was the way things were supposed to be.

44

Some of the women even thought the men were right, and that their ideas were as things were supposed to be. And slowly, the men took control of all of life. Until the women were left with freedom only within the Society of Women itself.

The men began to give orders to the women, and to say which man their daughters would marry. The men began to insist that inheritance should not come through the women at all.

And then, when things were not at all as they ought to be, a thing happened that is still spoken of among the women of the society.

Tem Eyos Ki went to the waiting house to pass her sacred time in a sacred place, sitting on moss and giving her inner blood to the Earth Mother. Men were not allowed near the waiting house, it was too sacred for them to understand or approach. And Tem Eyos Ki stayed in the waiting house with some of the other women whose time it was, and she was there for more than four days.

When she came from the waiting house she was a woman hit by lightning, a woman struck by wonder, a woman shaken with power, a woman filled with love. She walked from the waiting house with a look on her face more potent than magic. Seeds of life glittered in her hair.

She smiled, and sang a song that told of love that knew no limits, of love that knew no bounds, of love that demanded nothing and expected nothing but fulfilled everything. She sang of knowing and trusting, of sharing and giving. She sang of a place so wondrous the minds of people could not even begin to imagine it. A place without anger or fear, a place without loneliness or incompletion.

She walked through the village singing her song, and the women followed her. They collected their children, boys and girls alike, and followed Tem Eyos Ki, leaving behind the cooking pots and weaving looms, leaving behind the husbands and fathers.

Tem Eyos Ki walked past the village, along the beach, toward the forest, singing her song of love and wonder. And the women followed.

The men found the village empty, the meals uncooked, the work unfinished. They followed the women, angry and threatening. They followed the women into the forest. Followed the women who followed Tem Eyos Ki, who followed the song she learned in the waiting house when she found love.

Storm wind tried to stop the men with gales and rain. The forest tried to stop them. Even the sky tried to stop them with thunder and lightning and the sea smashed herself against the rocks to warn the women.

The women wept and said they did not want to return home. The men threatened to kill Tem Eyos Ki. To silence her song so that she would never again tempt their women from their hearth fires. They went after Tem Eyos Ki to kill her.

But Qolus, who is a female figure and was father of the four sons who fathered all ordinary people, sent a magic dugout, and Tem Eyos Ki leaped into it, still singing her song. She flew above the heads of the shouting men and the weeping women and sang of things people had forgotten. The storm stopped, the wind calmed, the rain stopped falling and the sea became still. All creation listened to the song of Tem Eyos Ki. And then she flew away.

The men stopped arguing and began to talk. The women said why they had wanted to leave. The men listened. The women listened. They went home together, to try to live properly again.

But sometimes a woman will think she hears a song, or thinks she remembers beautiful words, and she will weep a little for the beauty that she almost knew. Sometimes she will dream of a place that is not like this one. Sometimes she almost thinks she knows what it was Tem Eyos Ki was singing in her song. And she weeps for beauty she never knew.

THE WOMEN'S SOCIETY

And then the world turned upside down.
Strange men arrived in dugouts with sails
that smelled terrible and were infested
with bright-eyed creatures the like
of which had never been seen on the Island.

P EOPLE WERE LIVING almost as they were intended to live. Almost. And the Society of Women was strong. It was inter-tribal, open to all women, regardless of age, social status, political status, or wealth.

No woman could buy her way into the society. No woman could inherit a position in the society. Each member of the society had been chosen by the society itself, and invited to join and become one of the sisters. Even slave women could belong to the society if they were invited, and their owner could not deny them the right to join, nor keep them from the meetings, nor forbid them permission to join in the ceremonies, for the society was powerful, and respected by all.

The education of all girl children was the duty of the members of the Women's Society. They taught with jokes and with songs, with legends and with examples, they taught the girls how to care for and enjoy their bodies, how to respect themselves and their bodily functions, they explained to them all they would ever need to know about pregnancy, childbirth, and child care.

And then the world turned upside down. Strange men arrived in dugouts with sails that smelled terrible and were infested with sharp-faced bright-eyed creatures the like of which had never been seen on the Island. These men wanted water, and food, they wanted trees for masts, they wanted women, for it seemed as if they had none of their own. Their teeth were pitted and black, their breath smelled, their bodies were hairy, they never purified themselves with sweating and swimming, and they talked in loud voices. They wanted otter and seal skin and were willing to pay with things such as the people had never even dreamed.

And the world turned upside down. People got sick and died in ways they had never known. Children coughed until they bled from the lungs and died. Children choked on things that grew from the sickness in their throats. Children were covered with running sores and died vomiting black blood. Nobody was safe. Not the slaves, not the commoners, not the nobility, not the royalty. Entire villages died of sickness or killed each other in the madness that came from drinking the strange liquid the foreigners gave for seal and otter skins.

And then new men arrived. Men who never talked to women, never ate with women, never slept with women, never laughed with women. Men who frowned on singing and dancing, on laughter and love. Men who claimed the Society of Women was a society of witches.

"Thou shalt not suffer a witch to live," they insisted, but the people would not allow them to kill the women of the society.

Instead, the priests had to be content to take the girl children. Instead of being raised and educated by women who told them the truth about their bodies, the girls were taken from their villages and put in schools where they were taught to keep their breasts bound, to hide their arms and legs, to never look a brother openly in the eye but to look down at the ground as if ashamed of something. Instead of learning that once a month their bodies would become sacred, they were taught they would become filthy. Instead of going to the waiting house to meditate, pray, and celebrate the fullness of the moon and their own bodies, they were taught they were sick, and must bandage themselves and act as if they were sick. They were taught the waves and surgings of their bodies were sinful and must never be indulged or enjoyed.

By the time the girls were allowed home to their villages, their minds were so poisoned, their spirits so damaged, their souls so contaminated they were not eligible for candidacy in the Society of Women.

The boys were taken away, too, and taught that women were filthy, sinful creatures who would tempt a man away from his true path. They were taught women had no opinion that counted, no mind to be honoured, no purpose other than to serve men.

In less than a generation the world turned upside down and all reason and truth flowed out and was nearly lost.

The elder sisters died with tears in their eyes because the young women were not prepared to learn how to love their own bodies.

Who cannot love herSelf cannot love anybody
who is ashamed of her body is ashamed of all life
who finds dirt or filth in her body is lost
who cannot respect the gifts given even before birth
can never respect anything fully.

The priests thought they had destroyed the matriarchy. They saw fighting and drunkenness where once there was love and respect. They saw men beating their wives and children. They saw mothers beating their children and even abandoning them. They saw girls who should have been clan mothers become prostitutes in the cities the invaders built.

They did not see that a few women saved and protected the wisdom of the matriarchy, even at the risk of their lives. Meeting in secret, often in the churches of the invader.

Pretending to believe what the priests taught. Being very careful of what they said, guarding jealously that which they knew.

Much was lost. Much will never be regained. We have only the shredded fragments of what was once a beautiful dance cape of learning. But torn as it is, fragmented as it is, it is still better than the ideas the invader brought with him.

A few women, old now, and no longer strong. A few elder women who kept alive what the invader tried to destroy. Grandmothers and aunts. Mothers and sisters. Who must be honoured and cherished and protected even at risk of your own life. Who must be respected. At all times respected. Women who Know that which we must try to learn again. Women who provide a nucleus on which we must build again. Women who will share with us if we ask them. Women who love us.

And there are young women now, some of them unlikely seeming candidates, who have been tested and found worthy, and who are learning the old wisdom. Young women who do not always manage to Do what they Know, and so need our love and help.

The dance cape is not complete, the song is not finished, the dance is not entire, the words are not all known. But the need is now and Old Woman is with us, and will help us and come to us when we most need her.

CHESTERMAN BEACH

"They came outta the fog,
ships like nothin' we'd ever seen before,
and then, like ducklings around their mothers,
boats and men pullin', comin' toward the beach
wavin' and yellin' happily, as if the smoke
from our houses was the nicest thing
they'd seen in months . . ."

W E WERE ALL sitting around on the front steps pay-
ing more attention to Nothing than to Something,
watching the fishboats and pleasure boats and
yachts heading home, and listening to radios. Plural. What
we do most nights is move the radio near an open window
and sit outside where it's at least fresher, if no cooler, and
then the other people move to their steps with their radio
near a window, and then some more people, and that way
nobody has to crank up the sound to where it's a pain in the
ear and everyone can hear the news. Of course, if one
dedicated individualist tunes into a different station, that's
kind of it for communication through sociability but seeing as
how we don't have a whole lot of choice about stations, there
isn't much worry except from tape decks and more and more
of us have them now, in spite of about as rotten lousy a
fishing season as we've ever had. Which is why there were so
many of us sitting listening, a lot of us figured that the dozen
and a half or so fish we'd been hauling in weren't worth the
cost of the gas it took to go get them so there were lots more

pleasure than fish boats out on the chuck. Billy Peters, he'd even gone so far as to get four of the elders to stand on deck playing drums and chanting, the way they used to in the old days, and when that didn't do anything but give everybody a thrill and make the old men feel real good, the rest of the people figured they might as well just sit'er out, because when there's no fish out there, there's no fishing either.

So we're sitting sipping our after-supper coffee and the voice of the CBC announcer came rich and fruity from the radios, telling all the listeners that the entire coast was on a red tide alert and the taking of all clams, oysters and mussels was prohibited.

One of the boys snickered and said, "Red Tide. Hell, that's for the white boys," and a couple of others laughed and nodded, but my Granny shook her head and sucked her top teeth, and that's all she did. But Fred, he went in the house and shut off his radio and came over to sit on our steps, and then Frank and Jackie and Jim came over so I went inside and turned off our radio and got out the big enamel kettle and put it on the gas ring to boil for tea.

Angie Sam brought over a double batch of oatmeal cookies she'd just pulled from the oven and Alice and Big Bill brought a batch of brownies, and before the water was boiling, what with rolls and pies and buns and Christie's spice cake, and some other stuff that got mixed up elsewhere and put in our oven to bake for later, well, we were set for a good evening.

The big surprise was when my Granny said I should maybe take notes so I could write it all up later and then for sure the story wouldn't be lost when she died. For years my Granny has been matter-of-factly talking about when or after she dies, not because she's puny, or sickly, or morbid, but because for her and a lot of the old people, dying is as much a part of living as being born, and it's an important thing, a big step, and not something to be taken lightly. But this was the first time she'd as much as Told me to write stuff down. Usually I have to ask permission and lots of times she just says No, writing's for those too lazy to remember, and until I have permission, it wouldn't be right, so I've got a headful of stories if she ever says it's okay to write them down. I got out my notebook, but mostly I used my ears, which is what I've sort of been trained to do, I guess, by a lifetime of living and studying with her.

"We didn't call it Red Tide", Granny said softly, in English because so many of the young people don't speak good Nootka and some of them don't speak any at all. We all sort of leaned forward to hear better and she told us the name in Nootka, but there's no use trying to write it down here because we've got no alphabet, we never needed one, we memorized all the important things, and even if I found a way to spell what Granny called Red Tide, you'd only be able to guess at the pronunciation anyway.

Not all of us memorized everything, of course. Some people were interested and memorized family ties by birth and marriage, some memorized trade and fishing right agreements, some memorized songs and chants for navigating by sea current, some memorized the words of songs or poems, or the steps of dances. Of course it's a risky way to do it. Each smallpox or tuberculosis epidemic carried off chapters of what had been a real living history. But they told me at school the big library at Alexandria burned flat to the ground, so maybe when it's time for rotten luck it's time for rotten luck.

Red Tide is caused by little living things in the sea, plankton maybe, and it flourishes in sunlight and warmer water. The water off the island is never what you'd call Warm, but everything is relative and summer is warmer than winter, water and all, and these little things grow, and they multiply, and sometimes there's so many of them they stain the water with the colour of their massed bodies. If oysters, clams, or mussels strain this water through themselves and ingest these little things, well, it doesn't make them sick, but anybody eating them is going to get sick and probably die.

"From the time all the salmonberries are ripe, past the time all the blackberries are picked, through the time of the oolichan run to the first frost," Granny half chanted, "nobody

53

who wants to stay clean will eat of the female-appearing shellfish." If you don't know what Granny meant by female-appearing shellfish, well, take a good look for yourself sometime. Those milk weed pods are tame alongside a big blue mussel once she's been opened.

"Those who eat what is restricted may never suffer in this life, and nobody can say what price they'll pay in the next life, for it's not for us to know that. But many who break the religious food laws will die and there's no protection or cure. First a tinglin' in the fingertips, then around the lips and face. Tinglin' will become numbness. The numbness will spread and become paralysis. There is no pain. There are even soft sensations and brightly coloured dreams, but the soul slips away as the intoxication takes hold and then the breathin' stops and the body is a hollow shell. Just dead meat over bones held together in a bag of skin."

There was a bit of silence, and then the young fellow who'd said Red Tide was for the white boys took a deep breath and said, not looking at Granny, "I never knew anyone who died from it."

"I do," she said just as softly, and she whispered a few names and said some holy words. "A whole family: mother, father, five little kids. The parents were taken young and raised in residential school and never taught our ways. And they had a feed of clam chowder one night in the summer and in the mornin' when there was no sign of anyone, someone went over to check and they were all dead, and the leftover chowder sittin' in a bowl — white on the inside, blue on the outside — and we took the chowder, bowl and all, and buried it with the chowder pot she'd boiled it in, but it was too late."

"Used to be," she accepted a cup of tea and the lemon tart Sammy Adams gave her, and after she'd blown on her tea to cool it a bit, eaten the tart and nodded her satisfaction, then rinsed her mouth by drinking the tea, she handed back the cup for a refill and started over again. "Used to be if there was a bay or cove full of redstain the news would get around pretty fast. Like, if we spotted one here, we'd send message dugouts to Queens Cove, Zeballos, Nootka Island, Kyuquot, all our family tie villages, and we'd tell them. They'd send messages to other places and then them places would warn others, and soon we'd all know. And maybe we'd mark the place with a carved warnin' board or post and for four years — four years without redstain — nobody would eat from there."

"But there were times the poison food was put to sacred use. Some of the things it was used for are still secret," and we all nodded, respecting the secret. "The old woman and some disciples would go and gather up a mess of infected shellfish and then they'd take'em home and boil'em until what they had was a real thick soup, boiled until most of the water was gone. And they'd dry and mash it up, and put the whole mess in the sun to evaporate, and what you'd have, after it was pounded good, was like a powder. And if you mixed it with water, well, you had poison."

She smiled a small satisfied smile to herself, and looked out over the water. "One'a Captain Cook's sailors died from redstain. Maybe more than one, but one for sure."

"They teach in school that Cook found this place. Well, he wasn't the first. He just got the credit because he was English and the English never did like to admit to bein' second to anyone. There were lots of Spaniards here first. A long time before the English, a couple of generations before the English. The story is, it was part of their religion, sort of, and they'd send out ships and crew lookin' for new worlds. Them that found somethin' and got back to report it was heroes and them that never made it back was angels, or somethin' . . . what's the word, Ki-Ki?"

"Martyr," I said quickly.

"Martyr," Granny nodded, drinking more tea. "Well, some of those martyrs came here." She giggled suddenly, her face sort of falling into all her wrinkles, and I could see the little girl she'd been a long time ago. "Not too many of the heroes, but about three boatloads'a martyrs," and then the dried-apple grin disappeared and the soft face of my grandmother hardened until it was as if it was carved out of stone, the unyielding stone of the granite cliffs.

"Keestadores," she grated in a cold voice, "Keestadores, with metal on their bodies and metal hats on their heads, and no heart at all worth talkin' about," and we all sat still, feeling all kinds of things in the tone of her voice.

"They came outta the fog, ships like nothin' we'd ever seen before, and then, like ducklings around their mother, boats, and men pullin', comin' toward the beach, wavin' and yellin' happily, as if the smoke from our houses was the nicest thing they'd seen in months. So we welcomed them, fed them, gave them fresh water to take back to their mother ship, and food for their friends still on board."

"At first things were okay, but bit by bit it all started to get ugly. They had officers and sailors and soldiers, but the trouble came from their holy men, the priests in their robes. Eyes like burnin' coals and not even the memory of kindness in them. They started off complainin' about kids swimmin' naked and wound up tryin' to control our lives. Wound up talkin' against the Women's Society, tellin' the men that women weren't supposed to be partners, weren't supposed to pass inheritance, were only there to be used by men, bossed around and traded like things."

"Seems everythin' about the women just stuck sideways in their throats. Don't know what their own women were like, never saw any of the Keestadore women, they only brought men and young boys who got used as women whether they liked it or not."

"And at first we shrugged, everyone does things different, but they didn't have the same attitude, they started tryin' to get us to do like they did. Their Sunday-best manners wore off real quick, and next thing you know they pointed their big gun at a perfectly good tree and blew it up, just to prove what they could do. And said there'd have to be changes or they'd use it on the village. Inside'a no time at all they were bein' a real bother."

"They might'a been satisfied with usin' boys when there was no women around but once they saw women, that's what they wanted. And while neither nobility nor royal women would go near them, some of the commoners and most of the slave women were willin' to trade personal favours for some of the strange things the Keestadores brought. But before long, every woman who'd been with the Keestadores that way got sick. Ugly sick."

She stopped talking for a long time, sat holding her cup, staring out at the water where the first night shadows were walking on the waves, and we all sat and waited, knowing she was hurting, remembering the shock and horror of the first encounter with syphilis and the murderous effect it had. Some of the women used the time to wipe sleepy faces and lie half-asleep little kids on my bed, where they popped thumbs in mouths and closed their eyes, feeling safe, knowing they'd get taken home when it was time. Some of us lit up those little green coils from Italy that keep the mosquitoes away, and I took Granny her shawl and made another big pot of tea and then we all settled down to hear some more of the history nobody ever puts into school books. We've heard the other side of the story so often some of us even believe it.

When Granny asked for more tea we knew she was ready to go on, and we re-grouped ourselves and watched the bay and the islands as they are now and, at the same time, as they must have been all those years ago before the logging companies came.

"One day the women called a meeting and said they didn't want no more Keestadores and no more interference or foolishness from them or their priests. And when the old woman told what the rottin' sickness was doin' to the women who'd been with the sailors, and described how ugly the whole business was, everyone agreed that hospitality might be one thing, but the lines have to be drawn someplace, and babies born without noses or with teeth all sharp-pointed like a cat's is plenty of reason to draw the line."

"So the council met with the Keestadores and let it be known we'd had enough. None of the Keestadores had learned any of our language, but some of the Memorizers had learned enough of theirs to get the message across. And they didn't like what they got told."

57

"We didn't cut'em off from the water or tell'em they couldn't fish no more, but we did put our villages outta bounds. They objected and for a while we hadda make sure the Fighters were easily seen, with their big war clubs handy, and at first we moved all the mothers and children back into the bush in case they did the thing with the big gun they'd been threatenin' to do."

"The Keestadores finally moved on a-ways, and they didn't use their big guns, but they was still hangin' around and still a lot of trouble. They'd come as close as they dared to the village and try to smile and sweet-talk and when that didn't work there were some dirty looks and some pushin' and shovin' and it got so's before we went to bathe and purify in the warm sulphur springs we'd have to send twenty or thirty Fighters in to shift them others."

"One day we found one of the Fighters with half his head blown away and we knew the Keestadores done it, but we didn't know which one'a them, and we knew sure by then they'd all lie about it and the one that done it would be protected by his friends and nothin' would come of makin' any fuss, and we figured maybe they'd just leave us alone. Some of the other Fighters were real upset, a soul that dies unavenged don't rest easy, but mad as they were they knew it just wasn't Time. You gotta wait until it's Time."

"Then one night we were all listenin' to a poet tell the new story about the sea and a makebelieve trip to a magic land, and we heard a god-awful scream. We all ran around tryin' to find out what it was and all we found out for sure was there was two girls missin'. Little girls, ten and eleven. They'd been goin' to get the stuff for basket makin'. One of them was learnin' how and wanted to show the other, and work on it while listenin' to the poet, and her friend had gone along with her to keep her company. But even though we looked all night we didn't find'em. Until first light. Then we found'em."

She didn't raise her hand to wipe away the tears, she just let them flow down her face and fall to darken the front of her blue cotton dress. Her voice trembled but she just kept talking, almost chanting, and I figured she had to keep things inside some kind of structure or she'd just come apart with the pain of it.

"The first was found face down, floatin' half in half out of the water, her legs bobbin' in the waves, her eyes open and starin' blind at the sand and rocks of the beach. Her dress was found later. Her body ws covered with bruises an' bites, her little girl breasts were scratched and chewed, but the sea had washed the blood away. A piece of cloth shoved in her mouth had stoppered her cries and there were blue fingermarks on her throat. But what had killed her was havin' the back of her head crushed, maybe by a rock, maybe by the handle of a Keestadore sword. She was dead when they chucked her in the water, but her last hours had been hell and death come as a friend to her."

"The second was found in the bushes, lyin' on crushed salal, surrounded by huckleberry and Oregon grape. Naked. We never found her dress. They'd took their time with her and there was tears dried on her face, and places where the dust and dirt of her struggle was washed away by her cryin'. Her mouth was bruised, her lips cut and split and there was a big bruise on the right side of her face."

"The people had no way of understandin' what had happened. There'd never been anythin' like this in all the time since the beginning of life, and so they could only stare at the proof of horror and feel numb shock. They could see what had been done, but they couldn't understand how, or why. It had been hard enough to believe the Keestadores would force a grown women to have sex when she didn't want, but the thought of sex with a child was just too horrible for the people to even imagine, so they didn't know what to think. The old woman examined both the babies, and it was as if the sure evidence of what she found shook the centrepost of all creation, and threatened the here and now as well as the past and future, and she spent a long time alone in her sacred place, prayin' and askin' for help from the magic sources, help in understandin'. When she finally told us what she had learned from the prayers and magic, we believed her, but we still couldn't understand why anybody would want to do a thing like that."

"We didn't let the mothers of the girls near them until we'd washed and fixed them up, and nobody wanted to tell them what the old woman said had happened. Lots of us cried or was sick — or both — just thinkin' of what them babies had been through. Nobody wanted to think about it and nobody who knew could stop thinkin' about it, and everybody was . . . was just numb. Just numb."

"Some of the Fighters was all set to just wade in and let fly, but we cooled them down by pointin' out they'd never get'em all and the survivors would still have them big guns, so we waited."

"Waited and never said a word. Never even told'em two babies had gone over."

"The Keestadores had a camp down a fair piece from the village, with a boat out on the bay. They'd moved their horses off'a the boat and had a fenced-off place for them at night but durin' the day they let'em roam around pretty loose. There were guards posted at night to make sure nobody snuck up on'em, and patrols durin' the day."

"Some of the disciples and initiates met at the waitin' house and spent a time with old woman, prayin' and fastin' and meditatin'. And then half a dozen of them, sisters whose names are known only to the disciples and spoken only with love, went to the place where the Keestadores were. And one by one they chose a sentry and went walkin' up, smilin' as bold as you please, friendly and invitin'."

"You gotta remember, we didn't have no whores or floozies, these women were initiates of the Society of Women, students of Old Woman, like Ki-Ki is, proud of their bodies and knowin' they were clan mothers in the makin', and not one of'em had been near a Spaniard that way before. Not one of'em would'a gone near a Spaniard ordinarily."

"Them sentries thought sure they'd been blessed by their god! They'd never known women raised to be proud of, and to enjoy, their bodies and all good feelin's. Inside of a couple of nights, guard duty was somethin' they was lookin' forward to and the ones not on sentry duty would grin and feel jealous about each sound from the shadows. Rustlin' of grass and sighs and moans and sometimes a surprised yell endin' in the deep throat laughter of a teasin' woman."

"Well, the tide was low, real low, and that meant there was only one way in or out of the bay because a sand bar blocked the other way. There was an early fog rolled in after the sun went down and the ones on shore lit a big fire to push away the damp and the scarey shadows."

"The dugouts came through the fog, movin' real quiet. Fighters from Tahsis, Kyuquot, Clayoquot, from Hesquiath, Yuquatl and Hecate, from villages that don't even exist any more because the epidemics killed'em all. From Ehatisaht and Kelsemaht and Opitsaht and Kallicum."

"Men and women pullin' the paddles, men and women who'd purified themselves and were ready to die or kill, men and women who'd faced their own fears and got past'em, and were ready now, if need be, to face the unknown of the other world."

"And on shore the sacred sisters walked out of the fog smilin', their bare breasts glistenin' with clarified seal oil, their skins perfumed with hemlock and bracken, their hair scented with the juice of flowers."

"Fog isn't solid like a wall, it blows and drifts, and where it's blown away the moonlight shines and the sentries seen the sisters movin' toward'em and they started takin' off their metal helmets and the metal on their chests and back, barin' their skin to the night air, to the touch of the sisters."

"The dugouts drifted in past the point and spread out in the fog bank, blockin' the passage. The women slid over the side, their bodies thick with whale oil against the cold of the water. Every fourth woman had a stone bowl full of burnin' coals, with a wet cedar basket over the top to hide the glow. The other three had seal bladders full of melted seal oil, or cedar pitch, and they swam real quiet up alongside the big wooden ship and they started smearin' her all along and above the water line."

"The sacred sisters smiled and moved close to the sentries and let themselves be touched and stroked and coaxed into lyin' down on the ground. Them sentries got a real surprise when the sisters locked their legs around the sentries' waists and crossed their ankles behind the sentries' backs and fastened their mouths tight on the sentries' lips to smother all sound. Because then they used their knives to slit the Spanish throats."

"When the sentries quit thrashin' and twitchin' the sisters rolled out from under'em and pulled on the Spanish helmets, breastplates and backplates, then stood in the wispin' fog, the blood, Spanish blood on their bodies, coolin' and dryin'. To the Spanish grouped around the fire, everythin' looked okay. The few little noises they'd heard only made'em grin and wish they'd been on guard duty and they couldn't see clear because of the fog and because they were so close to the big fire that their eyes couldn't focus in the dark anyway."

"The sisters made shrill whistle sounds, like 'skeeter hawks, and the army moved in from the woods, movin' quietly, slippin' from shadow to shadow, from fog trace to fog trace, keepin' rocks'n'logs between them and the ones gathered around the fire listenin' to a musician playin' music from their home place. People from what's now Tofino'n'Bamfield'n' Ucluelet'n'people of the Tse-Shaht who'd come down the canal, and people from just about everywhere around here. All the men and even some boys who hadn't quite finished their manhood trainin', and women who weren't pregnant or nursin' a child. Only the old ones, the young ones, or women with little kids weren't ready to fight."

One of the fellows looked confused, so Granny quit talkin' and waited for him to either figure it out for himself, or ask. He asked. "I didn't know women were warriors, too."

"Women fought," Granny sounded real patient and not at all put out about being interrupted. "Before the outlanders came, we didn't fight much at all, but when it happened, all the able-bodied got into it. Except the ones who couldn't be harmed, the special or sacred ones like the dreamspeakers, or memorizers, dancers, clowns, and women carryin' or nursin'

"Not all of our dead got brought home to be buried. We had a ceremony on the beach for them taken, or washed away by the sea. When a soul dies in sin, or unavenged, it doesn't rest, it stays and haunts the place. And what was evil in life is evil after, so we hadda leave some others who'd been strong and good in life to run herd on the Keestadore ghosts. Sometimes at night you can see them on the beach, caught in a fight as been goin' on for three hundred years, and there's some as can't sleep on Chesterman because part of their past is still fightin' there, and some as can't think straight while they're there, and others just feel real sad and don't know why."

"When we all got home, it still wasn't finished. The sisters who'd fooled the sentries had known before they did it that there was no chance they'd escape the rottin' sickness. We didn't have no way to cure it, and they knew that, too."

"They went to the house near the waitin' house and prayed. The Keestadore blood still stained their skins. And the people came to visit, but nobody touched'em. We smiled, and sang, and shared time, but we never touched'em. And Old Woman made her presence known and the old woman, she mixed up some of the redstain soup powder stuff and the sacred sisters drank it and got a bit affected. They laughed and made a couple of bad jokes, and lay down on their beds and drank more. And people kept talkin' and singin' and tellin' stories, and the sisters got dreamier and drank more of it, and soon we knew they were somewheres else, somewheres with bright colours and new music and good feelin' air, and then, almost all at the same time, they crossed over and left their meat behind on their beds."

"Some of us was cryin' real bad. These should'a been memorizers and teachers and mothers, and lived a long time. They were the best of us, and all of'em dead. One dead on the beach from a bash on the back'a the head, and the others from redstain."

"We picked up their beds so we wouldn't have to touch'em, and took'em to the beach and piled cedar logs and stuff, and lit'em up, and sent their clothes and treasures with'em. The one killed on the beach got brought back and burned, too, but not all of her soul come with her — part of it's still out on the beach. Night and day we fed the fire, and on the mornin' of the fourth day we let the fire die out, and that night, as the sun was goin' down, we all took baskets and filled'em and took the ash to the sea and scattered it, and went back again and again, the songs and prayers and chants and speeches goin' until all the ash was scattered."

"And we remember their names even today."

Granny sat in her chair staring out at nothing, and we all got up and left her alone with the past and the sisters whose names are known only to those in the Society of Women.

The Lost Goldmine

*"Maybe it was because the Cowichan
were so gentle, or maybe it's just that
gold does that to people. . ."*

I T HAD BEEN gray and heavy all day, the fog hiding the
sharp slopes of old Catface, closing in on us until you
could hardly see the outlines of the house next
door, and then, just before supper time, the wind started to
blow with a vengeance, all the fog blew away, and the rain
came down on us, driving almost sideways, hitting the windows with a sound like handsful of sand, seeping in under
the doors and around the window frames while the screaming
wind tried to take the cedar shakes off the roof and move
them back into the forest where they'd been for two hundred
years before they got cut.

Radio reception wasn't fit to listen to, just static and hum-
ming noises, and one by one people drifted over to visit us,
bringing some tea bags or a few ounces of coffee grounds, or
maybe some cookies or fresh-baked bread, and we sat around
for a while playing cards and talking, and some of the people
worked on their knitting or their carving, or whatever it was
they did in their quiet times.

Granny was working on a cedar basket, her bucket of water on the floor by her feet, the cedar strands soaking, staying pliable. Her old hands are wrinkled and knuckles swollen and knotted now, but she still makes the best baskets on the coast, so fine and tight and even, the designs showing clear and sharp.

When she started to tell her story she didn't look at any of us, she kept her eyes on her work, and let the words fall softly into the quiet. We didn't have to listen, she wasn't trying to Teach us anything, she was just offering a story for anybody who wanted to listen. Sometimes strangers get uneasy talking to my Granny because she doesn't always look directly at them when she talks. When Granny looks at you, she fixes you with her deep black eyes until you feel like she's looking right into the inside of your head, but it isn't always polite to do that, it doesn't leave a person much privacy, and there are times we find it impolite to force even our gaze on someone. Also, Granny doesn't always look at you when you talk to her, so sometimes people who aren't from here think she hasn't heard them, but there isn't much goes on my Granny misses. It's just that she uses her ears to listen, not her eyes, so she doesn't have to look at you, she looks off at something else, or watches her hands, or maybe sits nodding at the floor, listening and giving you all the room you need to find words and express yourself.

We sat where we felt most comfortable, letting the wind scream at the roof and tug at the door. Once in a while someone would get up quietly and add another piece of alder to the fire in the big black stove with the worn nickel designs. When it's warm we have a gas ring for heating water or cooking, and there are full bottles of gas come in on the freight boat regularly, so we don't have to worry about running out of gas. But when it's cold or damp, like it is all winter and part of the autumn, we light a fire in the wood burning stove, and there's always lots of alder for fuel. The crackling of the fire in the stove made a peaceful sound that sometimes filled in the pauses between words as Granny wove her basket, and her story, which probably won't ever get into the history books in the schools and only survived for us to hear because other people, before my Granny was born, memorized it and told it to their students who memorized it and told it to younger people.

"Just about the same time the people up-coast were introduced to the Keestadores, the people down-coast met up with'em, too."

"Now there's some people say us Nootka are hard-nosed and belligerent, but them as aren't Nootka are always jealous of us as are, and their opinion doesn't count for much anyway. We're the singers, the Kwagewlth are the carvers, the Salish are the politicians. And the Cowichan are the philosophers. Real gentle people, most of the time, always able to look at two or three or all sides of a question and always willin' to study with and share ideas and stories with other people. They've got the reputation for the most poetic language on the coast, but I don't know because I don't speak any of it or understand it spoken to me."

"Maybe it was because the Cowichan were so gentle, or maybe it's just that gold does that to people. We had a lot of gold here, but we never mentioned it, not to keep it a secret, but because we didn't think it was good for anythin'. It won't hold a cuttin' edge, and there was more of it than there was of natural copper, so we figured the copper was the precious metal, and used it for jewelry and ornaments. Maybe the Cowichan thought the Keestadores, who seemed to know a lot about metal, might know what to do with the stuff, so they showed it to them and asked what it was good for, which makes me wonder about havin' a mind that always looks for new ideas. In no time at all the Cowichan were faced with a choice of slavin' in a gold mine or bein' dead from a Spanish sword."

"They cut and blasted a big hole in the mountain and started whippin' and beatin' people to get'em to haul out rocks and gold. Men, women, and all but the little bitty kids or the very old were workin', and the ones not workin' were penned up in the middle of the village and held hostage. Anyone did anythin' wrong, they got beat and the hostages got abused. A person might take a beatin' for herself, but when you know your sister or some little kid is gonna get beat if you don't behave, you think twice about tryin' anythin'."

"A couple of people tried to get away and let other tribes know what was goin' on, but what happened was so awful, and the small and the old suffered so much, they all decided it wasn't worth it, so the Keestadores had it pretty much their own way."

"There was a girl had been livin' with the Tse-Shaht, learnin' how their women caught babies and teachin' the Salish weavin' she'd learned from someone else, and she was on her way home when she noticed this big mess on the hill. She didn't feel good about it, and the Cowichan, they always respect their feelin's, so she got the pullers takin' her home in the dugout to pull into a small crik and stay outta sight for a while, and she snuck close and just let her eyes find out the story. She seen the Keestadores whippin' at people and takin' them up the path to the mess, and she seen how wore out the ones comin' back were, and she went back and got the pullers to turn around and take her back up-coast, fast."

"The Tse-Shaht, like the rest of us, had just found out about the two little girls when she got back, and everyone believed what she had to say. When the Chesterman thing was done and the sacred sisters honoured, the whole fleet headed south."

"On the way down, other bands and tribes joined. There were fast two-and four-puller sealin' dugouts goin' on ahead to tell the people that the fleet wasn't just on a raidin' party or tryin' to invade anyone's fishin' territory. As soon as they said why it was headin' down, people joined in, either because they liked the Cowichan or because they figured maybe they'd be next. And, too, I guess it's true some people just like a good fight."

"Half way down the sealers came racin' back to say there was a Keestadore boat headin' up and the fleet hid itself and had a long talk about whether to try to take'em now or later. At first everyone was so steamed up they were all for now, but then they figured there was sure to be some noise, and people would get hurt or killed and they needed all the Fighters they could get because gettin' the Cowichan out from under was the important thing, so they just lay quiet and let the big galleon go by, and they planned plans and dreamed dreams for later."

"They hid the dugouts again a mornin's walk from the village, and they snuk in real close and just watched. They saw the Cowichan taken up the mountain path, and they saw the others brought down, wore out and some with marks from the whips, and they planned, and figured, and prayed, and waited."

"That night they hid themselves on either side'a the path goin' up to the mess and when the Cowichan was brought up in the mornin', all the Fighters were ready. A Keestadore officer up front, and Keestadore guards along the file, and another officer bringin' up the rear. There'd be five or six or maybe ten Cowichan, and then a Keestadore with a whip slappin' at them, and then some more Cowichan, and another Spaniard, and like that all the way down the line."

"When the whole bunch had gone past the woman at the foot of the hill, why she stepped out real quiet. She knew there was no sense tryin' for the head because'a the helmet, and the back and chest was covered with armour, so she just grabbed the officer by his bearded chin, lifted his head and slit his throat before he could even gurgle, let alone yell."

"Of course the Cowichan weren't goin' to raise the alarm. They just kept walkin' up the mountain, actin' just like they always did, makin' sure she was hid from sight while she put on the Keestadore armor and took his place. If the officer at the front had turned around all he'd'a seen would have been the metal hat glintin' in the early mornin' sun, just like always."

"The next Spaniard in front of her, he got the same treatment when another Fighter stepped out of the bush, real quiet, and did the same thing to him. One by one, workin' from back to front, they slit the Spanish throats and put on the armor. When the officer looked around, everythin' looked just the same to him as it was supposed to, right up until his own chin was grabbed and the last thing he saw was his own blood spurtin'."

"The Cowichan knew where he kept his key, and how to use it to unlock the chains around them, and they did that, but didn't take'em right off, they wanted to arrive lookin' as close to normal as they could. They all hid knives and such that the Confederacy Fighters gave them, and when they got to the mess at the top of the path, they shuffled and kept their heads bent, and looked at the ground, same as always, and the Spanish guards moved forward to change wore out workers for fresh ones and it was all over in no time flat. All the Spaniards were dead, and their bodies all thrown in the hole in the hill."

"The rest of the Cowichan were unchained, and the Keestadore swords'n'armor were divided up, and everyone trooped almost all the way back down to the village again. They stopped and re-formed a pretend column of Cowichan. They had chains around them, but they weren't locked shut, and everyone had a knife, and a lot of reason to use it."

"One of the Cowichan chiefs snuk carefully down to his own house and went inside and got his family war club. He'd got it from his mother's oldest brother who'd got it from *his* mother's oldest brother, and it was somethin' every Fighter envied. It was as long as a tall man's arm, and so heavy only the strongest men could lift it, and it looked mean. It had been part of the root of an old arbutus tree, and there was a big rock in the end of it where the root had grown around it in the ground, a hundred years before it was undercut by a creek and toppled over with the roots pulled up out of the earth by the weight of the tree. The rock was as big as two fists clenched together, and all around it, set into the wood, were whales' teeth and some pieces of walrus tusk, so it crushed and stabbed and cut all at the same time. When he swung it, the wind swished between the rock and the wood, between the teeth and the tusks, and it screamed like an eagle does sometime."

"The Confederacy Fighters and the freed Cowichan were

right in the middle of the village when the Cowichan Chief came outta his house with his club held up, and he swung it, and it screamed for him and then he let out the most god-awful yell, and the fight was on and it was here-we-go time."

"Some of the Keestadores tried to get their boat underway but it takes a long time to get the sails up and they didn't have all the pullers they needed for the long oars that stuck out the sides and down to the water. They tried to make a fight of it with the big guns, but the dugouts were already too close. Some of the Fighters had stayed back with the dugouts and were waitin' just out of sight around the point, and when the yellin' and fightin' started, the navy came in at full speed, every puller sweatin' and keepin' the rhythm just exactly. They got in so close to the big wooden ships that the Spanish couldn't point the guns down enough, they fired right over the heads of the pullers and into the sea. The firelances did it to the sails, and then they just hitched cedar-bark ropes to the big boat and steered her on the rocks and let the sea do most of the work for them."

"The sailors and Keestadores on the wooden ship had to swim for it, but they didn't have a chance. The dugouts closed in on them one at a time, and the steersman or steerswoman just leaned over and bashed in the heads of the swimmers or sent a whalin' harpoon through'em."

"They took the Keestadore dead up to the mine and tossed'em inside, and then let the priests go in and pray over the dead. And while the blackrobes were prayin', the Confederacy used Keestadore powder to bring the hill down over the hole, buryin' the whole lot of'em in with the gold they'd wanted so much."

"But then they saw how raw the earth looked there, and they knew it would be easy to tell there was Somethin' there, and it wouldn't take much figurin' to know what, so they got the idea to hide the evidence and suck in that other Keestadore boat at the same time, and they lit fire to the bush."

"Some of the holy people were upset about that because cedar and hemlock are sacred and arbutus is blessed and balsam is holy, and destruction is a sin, but when people have smelled a lot of blood their brains go funny, and they lit the bush."

"Between the blast that sealed the mine and the smoke from the bush fire, the other Spanish boat came back in a rush. From where they were it must'a looked like the Keestadores was chasin' the Cowichan for water and stuff to fight the fire. They could see the other boat bust on the rocks, and of course they wanted to help, and with their attention turned to two wrong directions, they didn't see the navy dugouts until they were up close, and the big guns were no use again."

"It wasn't as easy to get the last big boat because the sails were already up, but they threw bladders of oil through the holes where the oars stuck out and sent fire arrows and lances in and started some small fires. Some of the dugouts were sunk this time, and the big wooden ship just rode right over'em, splittin' the cedar and crushin' and drownin' men and women. There were so many dugouts, and so many Fighters, and the fires were spreadin' and the sails were startin' to burn and the ship didn't have much room to manoeuvre in the bay and the smoke from the fire was makin' it hard to tell what was goin' on. Finally it was the same as before, the boat burnin' and people tryin' to swim to safety and not findin' any safe place, swimmin' in water red with blood, hearin' the chant of the paddlers comin' closer, and then not seein' anythin' at all, and all of'em died."

"Before anyone got to celebrate, the wind shifted and the Cowichan and the Confederacy had to get away or burn like the bush they'd set afire. They headed north in dugouts, and it was like the bush wanted vengeance. The fire crowned and chased after'em, sometimes missin' entire stands of timber, like around Nitinat, fed by the wind, leapin' from the top'a one tree to the top'a another, faster than a swift runner can move, and the heat so hot some of the small lakes boiled like pots on the stove and people who'd tried to find safety in them died of hot water and no air to breathe."

"Before it was over, a third of the island had been burned,

a lot of people were dead or homeless, and innocent animals who'd had nothin' to do with any of it were gone forever."

She put her basket work aside and got up from the sofa and walked to the bathroom. We made a pot of tea, and waited for her to come out and tell us some more. But when she came out of the bathroom finally, she didn't look at us or speak to us, she just went to her bedroom, went inside and closed the door. So we finished our tea, washed the cups and left them to dry on the countertop, then everyone else went home and I went to bed to listen to the wind howlin' and the rain splashin' and to think about what it must have been like long before my Granny's granny was born.

KLIN OTTO

*"There was a song for goin' to China and
a song for goin' to Japan, a song for the big island and
a song for the smaller one. All she had to know
was the song and she knew where she was . . ."*

W E WERE SITTING on the deck of Mabel Joe's fishboat, leaning against anything we could find to
lean on, the summer sun almost too warm on our
faces, the wind blowing our hair and tugging gently at our
clothes. Shaula's little girl Trina was sprawled on her blanket,
sound asleep in the shade of Big Bill's shirt. It was an
Hawaiian shirt, with bright green palm trees with red-brown
trunks against a red and yellow sky, and it billowed and
flapped above her. Peter, Big Bill's different looking son, got
him the shirt from a bin in the St. Vincent de Paul store in
Vancouver when he took his rabbits over to win all the
prizes at the Pacific Exhibition, and while I personally figured
it to be the ugliest shirt I'd ever seen, Big Bill wore it on
every possible occasion. Alice teased him sometimes about
even sleeping in it, and he'd just laugh and put his arm
around her and give her a bit of a squeeze and laugh again
and say "Well, if I do, you're the only one knows for sure,"
and then they'd give each other a quiet special little smile and
anybody watching would smile too, from them being so happy.

My Granny was sitting on the fishbox, her legs dangling down like a little kid on a too-big chair, swinging her legs slightly, tapping one foot rhythmically, her face soft, eyes dreamy, lips moving, making silent words only she could hear.

The soft steady sound of the engine drifted through the snatches of conversation like a tune on a radio nobody was listening to, and behind us the white wake from the twin screws bubbled up from the blue water and trailed back to the village like a path.

My Granny started singing, an old song from the days before fishboats or engines, from before compasses and printed charts, from before the strangers came out of the fog and things began to change. We listened and those of us who knew the Nootka words heard the names of places we'd never seen or even heard tell of before, descriptions of bays and coves, headlands and star constellations, of rivers and beaches, coves and fjords. We sat, everybody silent, and in spite of the warm day, I could feel and see goosebumps on my arms and legs. Then Granny quit singing and started talking, her voice rippling like water, her eyes fixed on something nobody else could see.

"They were fairskinned people with supernatural powers who had the ability to levitate," she said in her own language, "and they brought us the ceremonies of absolution and ecstatic revelation."

Then she smiled and focused her eyes on some of the young people who don't speak the language and she switched to English, some of the rippling water sound disappearing from her voice.

"Copper Woman was livin' alone when the magic people came from the skies, down the path the sun makes on the water, comin' in a dugout like nothin' any of us has ever seen. They stepped out of it but didn't touch ground, they floated like fireweed fluff until they got to where she was standin' starin' and nearly shakin' with fear, and then they settled to the ground, soft and gentle."

"She'd been alone a long time, she'd been lonely so long she had forgotten there was any other way to be, but she'd remembered what she knew and tried to stay strong inside."

"She showed the magic women the house she'd built with rocks and logs, near the fresh water stream where the fish came up to spawn in the pools, and she cooked food for them and never even wondered how they knew her language."

"They stayed with her, ate with her, fished and swam and danced with her and they taught her things she needed to know."

Granny started to sing again, and though I had heard the song before, I didn't know how to interpret the meaning of the words.

"She told them how she'd never been able to even think of goin' back where her home was because the stars here were set in different patterns, and they taught her a song and a rhythm and told her this place was home now. They told her she'd never be lost again, and they went with her in the dugout made from a livin' tree, and introduced her to their magic. They introduced her to Klin Otto."

"Klin Otto is a river in the ocean, a current of salt water that starts in one special place off a bay in California and runs in a set pattern up to one special island in the Aleutians. And Klin Otto, she never changes speed, and she never changes direction, and she's always there, now, until forever. The life span of a woman is 80 years; there have been 187½ lifespans since Klin Otto was revealed to Copper Woman, so you know that since Old Woman was grown at that time, she isn't quite 15,000 years old."

She sang some more, and we listened. The baby slept, with her index finger in her mouth, and the silly clown puffins fell over themselves to get away from the fishboat.

"Everythin' we ever knew about the movement of the sea was preserved in the verses of a song. For thousands of years we went where we wanted and came home safe, because of the song. On clear nights we had the stars to guide us, and in the fog we had the streams and creeks of the sea, the streams and creeks that flow into and become Klin Otto."

"The steerswoman stood at the front of the dugout and she tapped the beat of the song with her stick against the carved prow, and the pullers pulled to the rhythm, all at once, so many pulls on one side. Then they'd all switch at once and the paddles would hang in midair for a beat, then dig in on the other side, all together, all pullin', and the steerswoman singin'. When she wanted to know where she was exactly, even in fog or rain when you couldn't see the stars, she'd be able to figure it out. She had a rope, made of sinew woven and braided together a special way, and there were knots woven into it at regular spaces. The rope was attached to an inflated seal bladder of a special size and weight. The pullers would stop pullin', the dugout would move at the speed of the current and, still singin', the steerswoman would wait for a special line in the song, then she'd throw the bladder into the sea and count the knots as they passed through her fingers. That told her how fast the dugout was goin'."

"When she knew the speed of the current, plus how fast the pullers had been pullin', she could figure out in a minute where she was by the line she was singin' in the song."

"There was a song for goin' to China and a song for goin' to Japan, a song for the big island and a song for the smaller one. All she had to know was the song and she knew where she was. To get back, she just sang the song in reverse."

"The words of the songs and the words of the purifyin' ceremonies and the meanin' of the chants were all she needed to travel anywhere. And the songs found the whales for food and brought the whalers home."

"No woman would kill a whale. Whales give birth to livin' young, they don't lay eggs like fish. They feed their babies with milk from their breasts, like women, and we never killed them. The man who killed the whale never tasted whale meat from the time of his first kill until after he'd retired as a whaler. And neither did his wife, because he had to be purified and linked to the whale and the link was through his wife, by way of the woman's blood and woman's milk, and this was a promise made by Copper Woman, through the magic women, to the whales. No one linked to them will eat of them. It is a promise."

79

"Only certain women could marry whalers and whalers could only marry certain women and there had to be a bond between them that went deeper than the bond between man and woman, flesh and warmth, it had to be a bond of soul and spirit. If the bond got broken or the trust betrayed the whales wouldn't come, the people went without, and the whaler had to purify himself. If he didn't, or couldn't, the link stayed broken, and he was finished as a whaler."

"For a certain time before he went whalin', they wouldn't touch each other like man and woman, like husband and wife, and they prayed certain prayers and ate certain food and stored up their soul energy."

"Then they'd go to the sacred freshwater pool and they'd sing and dance and bathe in the water, and clean themselves with hemlock and fir, and slap their skins to move the blood fast in their veins, and they'd pray."

"Then the woman, when she felt her energy was high, would run to the salt chuck as fast as she could and sit in water up to her neck, and she'd watch the sea and pray."

"The man would stay on the beach and pray and direct his soul energy to the woman, to help, and she'd send part of herself out to the whales and the link would be made, to him through her, because of the blood and the milk.

"They'd go back to the village and he'd go off after the whale, and the whole time he was gone she'd lie in her bed and stay linked and not eat. And if he got killed, she knew it first, and sometimes she'd die, too. Not always. Sometimes."

Granny's foot stopped wiggling, her leg quit moving, and she looked up at us.

"We're nearly there," she smiled, and hopped down off the fishbox, stiffer than a kid, but looking like one.

"Do you know all the songs?" Big Bill asked.

"The sickness killed off the songs," Granny shook her head sadly. "So many people died. So many songs and stories and sea routes and histories. I only know a few of them."

Then she grinned and reached for the picnic basket. "But i can always find this place."

STONES

*"They brought her here. Copper Woman.
The magic women brought her here when
they came to make sure she was all right
after the flood . . ."*

W<small>E LEFT THE</small> boat anchored and came ashore in the rubber dingy, and dragged it up on the sand where it'd be safe. We didn't eat any clams or oysters because it was salmonberry and blackberry time, but we had potato salad and crab and smoked salmon and cold beer and if the Queen of England had been there she'd have been as stuffed full and lazy as we were.

But no way would my Granny let us sleep off all that good food and beer. We were all put to work with lard pails and water buckets, picking blackberries, because when my Granny makes jam, you pick until you don't care if you see another berry or bush as long as you live. Granny picked right along with us, and sometimes her mouth was as busy as her gnarled old fingers.

"We had things we had to do," she told Liniculla, Suzie's little girl, "and we hadda do'em, too. Learnin' to weave baskets and raincapes from cedar bark or from special grass, learnin' how to comb the little white dogs we had so their long fur could be spun and made into warm vests. Lots of things we hadda learn, boys and girls alike. And every day we had to get our bodies ready. So that when the time came to go from bein' a girl to bein' a woman, we'd be ready."

"Swimmin'. We did a lot of swimmin'. Winter and summer. Sometimes we'd get a rope around our waists and get tied to a log and have to swim and swim and swim without ever gettin' anywhere, just swimmin' until we were so tired we ached, but our muscles got strong and our bodies grew straight. And we'd run. Didn't matter if you ran fast or not, you ran, up and down the beach in your bare feet until your feet were tough and it didn't matter if you stepped on a shell or a barnacle or a sharp stick. Up and down, up and down, and just when we thought we were gettin' good at it they told us we had to learn to run without kickin' any sand."

"You try it sometime. Even walkin', the sand comes up from your feet and blows in the wind. Well, they showed us how to do it. Over and over they showed us how to do it. And we'd try. Just when we thought we'd never be able to do it, that it was impossible for anybody to do it, one of the sisters would run past, and there'd be no sand comin' up from her feet, and we'd start all over again. My back ached sometimes from tryin' to learn how to do it. And then one day, just like that, I could walk without sprayin' sand."

She laughed, looking down at Liniculla who was staring up at Granny, her soft girl-mouth half open, her dark eyes almost eating Granny's face.

"Then I had to start all over again, learnin' how to run. And you had to learn or you weren't a woman. It isn't easy becomin' a woman, it's not somethin' that just happens because you've been standin' around in one place for a long time, or because your body's started doin' certain things. A woman has to know patience, and a woman has to know how to stick it out, and a woman has to know all kinds of things that don't just come to you like a gift. There was always a reason for the things we hadda learn, and sometimes you'd been a woman for a long time before you found out for yourself what the reason was. But if you hadn't learned, you couldn't get married or have children, because you just weren't ready, you didn't know what needed to be known to do it right."

"So when I could finally run in the sand and not spray it all over the beach, I had to learn to do it backwards. You try that sometimes. You think you got good balance because you can walk on top of a fence and not fall off? You try runnin' backwards, see how much balance you got."

"And runnin' in water. First only to your ankles, so it dragged at your feet, and then deeper and deeper until you're in water halfway up your thighs, runnin' as fast as you can, and all that water that has to be pushed out of the way. Ki-Ki can do it, that's why she's got such nice legs."

"Of course," and she shot me a look with her sideways eyes, "it makes your bum stick out a bit, like a half a pumpkin on a plank, but that looks nice, too," and she laughed again and went to dump her berry-filled lard pail into the bigger water pail.

"When you'd learned everythin' you had to learn, and the Time was right, and you'd had your first bleedin' time and been to the waitin' house, there was a big party. You were a woman. Everyone knew you were a woman. And people would come from other places, uncles and aunts and cousins and friends, and there'd be singin' and dancin' and lots of food. Then they'd take you in a special dugout, all decorated up with water-bird down, the finest feathers off the breast of the bird, and you'd have on all your best clothes and all your crests, and you'd stand up there so proud and happy. And they'd chant a special chant, and the old woman would lead them, and they'd take you a certain distance. When the chant ended the old woman would sing a special prayer, and take off all your clothes and you'd dive into the water, and the dugout would go home. And you'd be out there in the water all by yourself, and you had to swim back to the village."

"The people would watch for you, and they'd light fires on the beach, and when they finally saw you they'd start to sing a victory song about how a girl went for a swim and a woman came home, and you'd make it to the beach and your legs would feel like they were made of rocks or somethin'.

You'd try to stand up and you'd shake all over, just plain wore out. And then the old woman, she'd come up and put her cape over you and you'd feel just fine. And after that, you were a woman, and if you wanted to marry up with someone, you could, and if you wanted to have children, you could, because you'd be able to take care of them the proper way."

"Every month, when the moon time came for you, you'd go to the waitin' house and have a four day holiday, or a party. Most of the women had their moon time at about the same time of the month, and you'd sit on a special moss paddin' and give the blood of your body back to the Earth Mother, and you'd play games, and talk, and if you were havin' cramps there was a special tea you could drink and they'd go away, and the other sisters would rub your back. We'd play Frog if the cramps were a bother. You scrunch down, like this," and Granny dropped to the ground to demonstrate "tuck your knees up under your belly, and put your head down with your forehead on the ground, and then you'd curl your back like a cat, like this, and breathe in deep, and then straighten your back. Looks funny, but it works. It's good when you first start havin' your baby, too, makes everythin' shift into the right place."

Liniculla dropped to the ground beside Granny and tried the position, and Suzie and I watched, looking at each other with quick looks, both of us blinking to keep from getting all watery-eyed as the girl who was years away from starting her menstrual cycle, and the woman who had finished hers years before, practised the cramp stopping position.

"That's right," Granny started to get up, a bit stiffly, "now you don't have to ever worry about gettin' bad cramps or havin' to take pills or anythin'. Just do the Frog game, and you'll be fine."

All this time Pete had been finding big clumps of berries just a few yards further on from where we were, and he'd call out, and we'd move toward them. Even talking to Liniculla, Granny would watch Pete, and from time to time

84

she'd grin a bit to herself. But she was deep in her talk with Liniculla and didn't speak to Pete, although we all knew Pete was listening to what Granny was saying. Finally Pete turned, and smiled, and Granny took an over-ripe berry and squished it against his nose.

"Some people," she teased him, "are so smart and so fast they're gonna meet themselves comin' back again. Come on then," and she took his hand and headed toward the circle of stones. We all put our buckets and pails down and moved fast to catch up with her.

"This one," she pointed, "was bigger before. Somethin' bust off the top of it, see, it's lyin' off to one side a bit. Don't know what it was broke it off. But I know it used to sit on top, all one piece. The sun ought to set right through that crack," and she pointed again, "and if it does, the moon'll come up between them two rocks and move over there before the sun starts to come up over that one."

She knew from the looks on our faces we hadn't understood anything but the words, so she sighed, and sat down on the grass and started to explain, as patient as if she was talking to a pack of two year olds.

"The circle isn't complete any more, and nobody knows where the missin' rock went. It was tall and thin and had magic marks on it, to measure with, and it didn't fall over or get dragged away. One time it was here, the next time it wasn't, just a bare patch on the ground where it used to be and no sign of it anywhere."

"The family that knew the full story of the measurin' rocks got the choke-throat sickness, the diphtheria, and what we know now is nothin' to what we used to know. We could measure anythin'. Days, months, years, distance, anythin'."

Pete lay back, staring up at the blue sky, his funny coloured eyes missing nothing of the cloud formations, his bleachèd hair blowing in the breeze. He just lay back, waiting for Granny to continue, and when she started talkin' in Nootka he understood what she meant. He didn't understand all the words, but he understood what the words were telling him. Granny's eyes got that far-away other-world look that meant she was seeing things the rest of us couldn't see, and Liniculla just stared at her as if watching Granny's face was like watching a movie screen that allowed her to see the hidden things, too.

"They brought her here. Copper Woman. The magic women brought her here when they came to make sure she was all right after the flood. She went out in her dugout to meet them and they lifted her, dugout and all, and brought her to this place."

"There are other places with other stones in other patterns, but they all do the same thing, they measure and mark. And the big one, the main one, is near where Copper Woman lived when she was a little girl, before she came here. When the magic women drew the design for her, she remembered the big rocks of her first home, and she cried, rememberin' everythin' she had lost."

"When they first got here, there were no rocks. Just sea and beach and a big empty field with grass and flowers. In the sand on the beach they drew a big circle and told her the secrets about it, and about how it's the link to the home, the real home, and when she was finished cryin' for her old place, they taught her how to do what they could do, lift up off the ground like dust in the wind, and when she could lift herself and float where she wanted, they showed her how to leave her meat and bones in her sack of skin and just send her Self someplace else."

"When she could do that, they told her how some bodies in the sky never change, and others do. And when she understood all that, they did their magic and they cut the rocks from the mountain and shaped them the way they wanted them, and then, the same way they moved themselves, they moved the stones and set them in place and marked them, and set the rock that's missin' now in its place, and put magic marks on it, and taught her everythin' about measurin' and how to use the measures and rocks to figure out distance and time."

"And with the rocks, and the stars, and the measurement, and Klin Otto, we always knew where we were and how much was ours."

"If she was so lonely for her own home," Peter asked softly, "and they knew where it was, why didn't they just take her home?"

"Why don't you just pick berries?" Granny grunted. "It's what we came here for."

CLOWNS

*"But mostly the clowns were very serious
about what they did. And the most famous clown
was a woman who wasn't even one of us . . ."*

I IT WAS COMING on Hallowe'en and the whole village was
getting itself involved. The people had stacked driftwood in a hollow square on the beach until it was too
tall for a man standing on another man's shoulders to add
anything more, and then they all set about filling up the
hollow centre with burnable junk, garbage, old newspapers,
whatever was lying around that would burn. We kind of
clean up the village every year this way. Every window had
a scary black cat or a big orange pumpkin scotch-taped to
it, and the closer it got to being the end of the month, the
more frantic the kids got in their search for costumes.
Liniculla was driving us all crazy. First it was a pirate, but
she decided her legs would get cold in the raggedy-bottom
cut-off pants, then it was a Princess, but she changed her
mind about that, too. I was just about ready to tell her to go
as a sack of spuds, and I had the sack to dump her into too,
when Granny put in her two-bits worth.

"A clown," she suggested.

"Everybody goes as a clown!" Liniculla shot that idea down in a rush. "Going as a clown means you couldn't think of a real costume to wear."

"Not a circus clown," Granny corrected quietly, "an Indian clown. Like in the days before the invaders came."

"We didn't have clowns, did we?" Liniculla asked, already making herself comfortable at Granny's feet, waiting eagerly for another story.

"We had clowns," Granny smiled and reached for the brush for Liniculla's long hair. "Not clowns like you see now, with round red noses and baggy costumes. Our clowns wore all different kinds of stuff. Anythin' they felt like, they wore. And they didn't just come out once in a while to act silly and make people laugh, our clowns were with us all the time, as important to the village as the chief, or the shaman, or the dancers, or the poets."

"A clown was like a newspaper, or a magazine, or one of those people who write an article to tell you if a book or a movie is worth botherin' with. They made comment on everythin', every day, all the time. If a clown thought that what the tribal council was gettin' ready to do was foolish, why the clown would just show. up at the council and imitate every move every one of the leaders made. Only the clown would imitate it in such a way every little wart on that person would show, every hole in their idea would suddenly look real big."

"It was like if you were real vain about your clothes, all of a sudden, the clown would be there walkin' right behind you all decked out in the most godawful mess of stuff, but all of it lookin' somehow like what you were wearin'. Maybe you had a necklace you always wore and showed off, well, the clown would have bits of bark and twigs, and feathers, and dog shit, and old broken clam shells, and anythin' else you can think of, and it'd all be made up in a necklace like yours. And if you walked a certain way because you were vain, the clown would walk the way you did. Where you had on your best clothes, the clown would be in rags and tatters and old bits of fern and you-name-it, and the clown's hair would look like a bird's nest, all mud and sticks and crap, and everywhere you went, the clown would go. Everythin' you did, the clown did. And nobody would ever dare blow up at the clown! If you did that, well, you were just totally shamed. A clown didn't do what a clown did to hurt you or make fun of you or be mean, it was to show you what you looked like to other people, let you see for yourself just how foolish it is to get yourself all tied in knots over some clothes and stuff instead of what counts, like bein' nice to people, and bein' lovin', and trying' to fit in with the people you live with."

"Or if you thought every word you spoke was gospel, the clown would just stroll along behind you babblin' away like a simple-mind or a baby. Every up and down of your voice, the clown's voice would go up and down until you finally Heard what an ass you were bein'. Or maybe you had a bad temper and yelled a lot when you got mad, or hadn't learned any self control or somethin' like that. Well, the clown would just have fits. Every time you turned around there'd be the clown bashin' away with a stick on the sand or kickin' like a fool at a big rock, or yellin' insults back at the gulls, and just generally lookin' real stupid."

"We needed our clowns, and we used'em to help us all learn the best ways to get along with each other. Bein' an in-dividual is real good, but sometimes we're so busy bein' in-dividuals we forget we gotta live with a lot of other people who all got the right to be individuals too, and the clowns could show us if we were gettin' a bit pushy, or startin' to take ourselves too serious. Wasn't nothin' sacred to a clown. Sometimes a clown would find another clown taggin' along behind, imitatin', and then the first one knew that maybe somethin' was gettin' out of hand, and maybe the clown was bein' mean or usin' her position as a clown to push people around and sharpen her own axe for her own reasons."

"But mostly the clowns were very serious about what they did. And the most famous clown was a woman who wasn't even one of us. She lived on the other side of the island with the Salish people. Or maybe it was the Cowichan, I guess I'm not too clear about that. Must be gettin' old. Anyway, this woman had been a clown all her life. Ever since she was a girl she'd been able to imitate people, how they walked, how they talked, so she was trained to do it properly for the right reasons, not just to get attention."

"The Christian people were dividin' up the island. This bunch got this part and another bunch got another part, and they built their churches and set about gettin' us into them. There's people say that it used to be the Indians had the land and the white man had the Bible, now the Indians got the Bible and the white man's got the land, and when you look at it, that's not far from wrong, except lots of us don't even got the Bible. Anyway, they'd built this stone church on a hill, with a cross on top of it pointin' up at the sky, and the preacher, he was gettin' people to come by givin' out little pictures and mirrors and such, things we didn't have. Might not seem like much now, a mirror, but they were as rare as diamonds, and it's bein' rare makes a thing worth a lot. Like roses are worth more than dandelions because there aren't as many of them, but they're both flowers."

"So the people started goin' to this church, and pretty soon it was just like the same old story. They started gettin' told what to do, and what to wear, and how to live, and this particular preacher, he was big on what they ought to wear. He didn't want the men wearin' kilts, he wanted 'em in pants, and he didn't want the women in anythin' but long dresses that covered 'em completely. And he kept tellin' everyone to learn to live like the white man, dress like the white man."

"Well, one Sunday didn't the clown show up. She was wearin' a big black hat, just like a white man, and a black jacket, just like a white man, and old rundown shoes some white man had thrown away. And nothin' else."

Liniculla giggled and her eyes sparkled, and Granny just kept brushing that long hair and telling her story.

"Well, the white preacher, he just about had a fit! Here's this woman more naked than not, walkin' into his church, and what's worse, the people in the church are all lookin' at her real respectful, not mockin' her or laughin' or coverin' their eyes so they wouldn't see her nakedness. And she moved to the very front and sat there and waited for the church service to start."

"Well, that preacher, he ranted and raved about nakedness, and naked women, and sin, and havin' respect for God, and then he came down from that pulpit and he grabbed ahold of that clown to throw her out on her bum."

"The people just about ripped him apart. You don't put violent hands on a clown! But the clown, she stopped them from hurtin' him, and then she went up to the front where he'd been, and she spoke to the people in their own language. She said we were all brothers and sisters because we all had Copper Woman as first mother, and were all descended from the four couples who left after the flood. And she said different people had different ways of doin' things, and that didn't mean any one way was Right or any other way was Wrong, it just meant all ways were different. And she said we ought to think how we'd feel if we were far from home, to put ourselves in the white man's place, how would we feel if there were only a few brown faces and lots of white ones, because maybe the preacher felt that way about bein' almost alone with us. And she said that just because he'd done a forbidden thing and got violent with a clown didn't mean that we ought to get just as mixed up and do a forbidden thing like get violent with a religious man. And she said we all had to find our own way in the world, we all had to find what was true, and what Meant somethin'. She said there was more than one kind of mirror. There was the white man's mirror that you got if you went to church, but there was the mirror in the eyes of the people you loved, and what it meant to them when you listened to someone who was so mixed up they'd do forbidden things."

"And then she walked out of the church and all the people got up and walked out behind her and left the preacher alone. And that church is still there today and it's still empty."

"Tell me more," Liniculla begged.

"Not without a cup of tea for my windpipe, I won't," Granny teased, and Liniculla ran to put the kettle on to boil. She rinsed out the teapot and warmed it up, and measured the tea carefully, then got cups and saucers, sugar and milk, and had everything all ready by the time the water was bubbling. Granny just sat watching her, smiling to herself, and it made me think of being ten myself and wanting to help, and how she always let me, even if it made more work for her. And after she'd had a cup of tea and was sipping a second, Granny started rocking slowly, and soon she was into a second clown story.

"The people were goin' down to Victoria a lot and tradin' with Hudson Bay for things they couldn't get anywhere else. They'd kill seal and otter, more than ever before so they'd be able to trade the skins, and even though everyone knew it couldn't last, even though everyone knew the animals wouldn't be able to survive, nobody seemed willin' to be the first to not do it. It was like they figured it was gonna happen anyway, they might as well get some of it for themselves. And not all of the stuff they traded for was worth anythin'. You make a long trip with a big bundle of furs, and you don't feel like bringin' it all home just because the Hudson Bay man doesn't want to trade for somethin' you want. More and more the company was just handin' out junk, and private traders were steppin' in with a few blue beads and lot of rum, and it was all a real mess."

"And this same clown woman, she took herself down to Victoria and she set up shop right next to Hudson Bay. Hudson Bay would give beads, so she had bits of busted shell. They'd give molasses, so she had wild honey. They'd give rum, so she had some old swamp water. And she just sat there. That's all she did, was just sit there. And the people goin' to Hudson Bay saw her, and saw the stuff she had to trade, and they knew what she was tellin' them. Some of'em went inside and traded anyway, but some of them just turned around and went back home, and some of them even went over and traded with her, and she treated them all real serious, took their furs and gave'em bits of shell and stuff, and they wore it same as they'd'a wore the beads."

"After a while the Hudson Bay man came out to see why hardly anybody had come to trade and he saw her sittin' there and he just about blew up, took himself off to the Governor and complained about the clown woman. The Governor, he took himself outside and had a look and then told the Hudson Bay man a thing or two, and from then on we got good tradin' stuff."

"The clown woman, she went home, and she thought about what had happened, and she decided that maybe the Governor wasn't such an ass after all. He knew what she was sayin', all right. She decided maybe she could get him to listen about the rum trade. The Americans were sendin' lots of ships up here, and they wouldn't trade nothin' but rum for furs. First they'd just put a small barrel of rum on the beach, free gratis, and then when the men were all into the rum, why the Americans would come and trade, and the result of that was pretty awful."

"The clown woman, she set off for Victoria again, and all the people knew she was gonna see the Governor and stop the rum trade. She didn't show up in Victoria, so the people went lookin' for her. Found her dead alongside her dugout, she'd been shot in the head."

"Hadda be a white man done it. We would never do violence to a clown."

Liniculla just stared at Granny for the longest time and even before she opened her mouth we knew that there'd be one little clown on Hallowe'en, all decked out in shells, and bark, and feathers and bits of stuff, trickin'n'treatin' all over the village, giving us all a chance to see things as they could be.

SONG OF BEAR

"There was a young woman who obeyed
all the laws of cleanliness, and
never went to the hills durin' her period, and
did all the things we're supposed to do,
but got loved by a bear anyway . . ."

I T WAS THE time of Suzy's menstrual period. It felt good to
be around a woman during her sacred time, good to be
able to smell the special body perfume, to share in the
specialness of it, expecting my own period to start any day,
wondering, as it seemed I always did, how it was that the
women of the village mostly all had their periods at around
the same time. Finally, since I had never been able to figure
it out for myself, I asked my Granny. She looked at me as if
she couldn't believe anybody could be so simple, and shook
her head gently.

"The light, Ki-Ki," she sighed, "it's because of the light. Used
to be, before electricity and strong light made it possible for
people to stay up half the night, that we all got up with the
sun and went to bed with the sun, and because we all got the
same amounts of light and dark, our body time was all the
same, and we'd all come full at the same time."

"I don't understand," I admitted, feeling more than a bit
dumb.

"Well, I don't either," she snapped, "I don't know if it's somethin' in our eyes, or our heads, or our bellies, or what. I only know that it's got somethin' to do with the light, and since everybody around here goes to bed at about the same time, and gets up at about the same time . . . do you understand how and why the geese go south? Then why do you have to understand this?"

She puttered around the kitchen for a few minutes, sucking her lip, making tsk-tsk noises with her tongue, shooting sideways looks at me, and then she smiled and sat down at the table with me, and took my hand.

"Used to be women weren't allowed to go up the mountain durin' their time. Because of the bears. Bears got big sharp noses, and they'd smell the blood of Womantime, and think it was a female bear, and try to mate. Prob'ly didn't intend any harm, but bein' hugged by a big male bear is a good way to wind up in bad shape. So the waitin' house was always protected from the bears, and women stayed out of the mountains."

"There was a young woman who obeyed all the laws of cleanliness, and never went to the hills durin' her period, and did all the things we're supposed to do, but got loved by a bear anyway. What it was, the bear saw her, and just fell in love. Just as soft, and sappy, and foolish as anybody is when love lightnin' hits her. The bear figured the young woman would be afraid, so it hid in the bushes and never tried to touch her or speak to her, it just watched. Watched with its little round eyes, and shook with love. Watched the young woman fishin' and watched her gatherin' berries. Watched her walkin', and watched her laughin' for days. Shakin' with love and feelin' there would never be any hope for this love."

"Well, one day the young woman came back from gatherin' food and she stopped at the freshwater pool and took a bath. Stripped off all her clothes, walked slowly to the pool, and swam around a bit. Stood in water halfway up her legs and bent over to wash her face. Lay back in the water and washed her hair. Stood up with her hair drippin' wet down her back, and rubbed her body with soft sand, and twisted this way, and twisted that way and then turned and looked right at the bush where the bear was hidin'."

"'I know you're in there,' the young woman laughed. 'I know you've been following me. Watching me. Scaring fish my way so I could catch them. You come out from that bush and let me see you.'"

"And the bear just about swallowed its tongue, but it stood up, sunlight glitterin' on its black fur, and it walked toward the freshwater pool, just as scared as anybody is when the one you love takes notice of you for the first time."

"'Come into the water,' the young woman invited, and the bear walked into the water, and they swam together, and they splashed each other, and the girl fastened her fingers in the bear's thick fur and the bear swam, pullin' the young woman easily. Then they lay in the sun to dry, and the bear stared at the young woman and wanted to touch her and love her."

"'I love you,' the bear managed, even though its voice was caught in its throat."

"'Why did you hide?' the young woman asked."

"'How could anybody as beautiful as you love a bear?' and a tear trickled from the poor bear's eye."

"Well, the young woman took the bear's head in her lap, and stroked its fur and kissed its nose, and said 'But you're beautiful. Strong, and gentle, and beautiful, and I do love you.'"

"'I'm a female bear,' the bear said.

"The young woman sat for a long long time and then she laughed and said 'If I can love a creature that looks as different from me as you do, why should I care if you are a male bear or a female bear? I love you, bear. I wouldn't not love you if you were skinny, or if you were fat, or if you were shorter, or if you were taller, because it's the love in you that I love, and the beauty in you that I love. Anyway,' the young woman laughed, 'meat and bones don't matter, it's what's inside them, the love spirit.'"

"And she stood up and the bear stood up and the young woman put on her dress, and took the bear's paw and walked

off with her, up the mountain to the cave where the bear lived, and they went inside and they loved each other. In the
cold winter they slept together and the bear's thick fur kept
them both warm, and in the springtime they came from the
cave together and danced, and fished, and were happy. And
the bear wrote a song for the young woman and would sing
to her, and the young woman was happy. And if people talked
about it, they talked about the wonder of a woman and a
bear livin' together and bein' happy, because the arrangement
of meat and bones doesn't mean anythin'."

And then my Granny sang the song of bear for me and
said I could write it down and share it. Anybody who can
find music for this song, and sing it, or dance to it, is a sister
of the bears and can ask to be admitted to the Bear Clan.
And when you go in the mountains, whether it is your
menstrual time or not, you wear a bell, so the bears will hear
you and know you are their friend.

The spirit of beauty
has come with me.
The spirit of beauty
has left her friends and family
to come with me.
Should her family come
and take her from me
I would die.

The spirit of beauty
walks with me.
I will gather berries for her
and tubers and roots from the hills.
I will bend myself to please her,
will dance for her, keep her warm.
I wrote this song for her
I sing it now for her

The spirit of beauty
has come with me.

98

QUEEN MOTHER

"When I was young they told me
if a generation of people got pushed to killin'
other people, it took four generations of peace
to get peoples' heads fixed afterward. And
we hadn't had them four generations . . ."

GRANNY WAS KNITTING a sweater for Liniculla, her big white plastic needles clicking together steadily, the thick natural wool smelling faintly oily in the warm kitchen, the Eagle-Flies-High pattern unfolding on the back of the sweater, black against the unbleached tan-gray of the main wool. Every so often she'd hold both needles in her left hand and with her right reach for, and sip from, the cup of wild rosehip tea she was drinking. Granny had sneezed getting out of bed that morning and had been flooding herself with rosehip tea ever since to ward off the cold she was convinced was trying to catch her. I told her she might save herself the cold at the expense of her kidneys, but she just muttered Nootka insults about cold pills and tiny-time-release and kept on guzzling her herbs.

Suzy and Liniculla had come over after lunch and Suzy tried to check Granny out, make sure she was still strong as a deer, but Granny just shook her off and said she didn't need to be fussed over, she just needed lots of rosehip tea. So we decided then and there to leave her alone before she got herself in a bad mood and told us all to leave the house for a few days.

"My grandmother was the Queen Mother," she said suddenly and flatly, replacing her cup and picking up her knitting again. "Her son was the king. She wasn't Queen Mother because he was the king, like in England. He was king only because she was Queen Mother. His son wouldn't inherit to be king. The Queen Mother's oldest girl, my mother, would become Queen Mother and *her* son — my brother — would have been king. I would have been Queen Mother after my mother because I was the oldest girl, and my son would have been king. Your mother, Ki-Ki, would have been Queen Mother, and if you'd had a brother, he'd have been king. Then you'd have been Queen Mother and your son would have been king."

"Only it all got buggered," she amended calmly, flashing a funny twisted smile at Suzy and me. "Got real buggered because the ships came back and instead of chasin' them away because of what had happened before, the people hoped this time things'd be different."

"Maquinna, he was maybe thirty when they came back. First the Spaniards, then the English hot on their tails, and already we knew about the Missions in California and explorin' ships sailin' all over everywhere lookin' for places to claim. Maquinna figured it was like swimmin' upstream against a flood. Salmon do it to spawn, but then they all die, so he talked about makin' the best of things and bendin' like a willow when the storms blow and, in spite of everythin', I expect he was right. When it's time for a thing to change, it's Time for a thing to change, and it changes."

"Things weren't all fine and easy any more anyway. When people get pushed to the point where killin' seems the only way, somethin' happens to them. They get jerked around inside somehow, and it takes a long time to get right again. When I was young they told me if a generation of people got pushed to killin' other people, it took four generations of peace to get peoples' heads fixed afterward. And we hadn't had them four generations."

"We came back from killin' off the Keestadores and burnin' a third of the island flat, and we were all more'n'a bit haywire. Seems like power does what booze does, just makes a person thirsty for more. The men had filled themselves with power, bashin' in heads and spillin' blood, and some of the women were the same. Families started lookin' on power as somethin' to have. Somethin' they needed. Power itself doesn't have to be bad, it's how you use it, I guess. Some of them still had guns they'd taken from Keestadores, and not all of the gunpowder got blown up in the mine."

"First it was little stuff, then it got worse. The Manhousats and Ahousats kept arguin' over fishin' rights and land measure. The family that knew the full story of the measurin' rocks and could'a settled the mess were missin' some of their people, so neither of the bunches arguin' would believe what they got told, and they said the story was incomplete. The next thing you know, they were at it for sure. Doesn't matter who started it or why, some say it was the Manhousats, some say it was the Ahousats, the end of it was the Ahousats wiped out most all of the Manhousats and moved to their island and they're still there."

"Raidin' parties went around the island and over to the mainland and up the big river to raid the interior people and bring home slaves and women. It was all pretty haywire all together, and the women they stole and brought down, they hadn't been brought up the same way, and that caused some trouble and hard feelin', too."

"Slaves had always been part of things, but they'd never been abused before, no more'n'a city person would buy an expensive horse and then starve it. A person didn't have slaves to do work, a person had'em to show there was food enough to feed'em. But that got buggered, too."

"There's people talk like it was pure paradise here before Cook came, but it wasn't. Prob'ly never had been. Sure not if you were a slave. The carvers who made the dugouts did the whole job while the tree was still standin', they cut the dugout out until it was just the top bit and bottom bit holdin' it to the tree. And they believed that the first thing the dugout touched, it would marry, so if it married the earth, it wouldn't float, and would go up on rocks tryin' to get back to what it married. So they'd lower it by pulleys and levers and such and roll it on wooden rollers all the way to the water. If it didn't ride right, or sunk when it touched water, the carver'd be so shamed he might kill himself. But after a while, just to show he was powerful and rich enough to afford it, a man would lay down slaves instead of alder poles, and run the big dugouts over them to the water, killin' and cripplin' them, and when the holy people said it was wrong, well, nobody listened."

"Then the dugouts came sayin' Cook was lost in the fog and they went out and steered him in to a safe place and gave him and his starvin' sailors food, and for their trouble, they got sick. The Queen Mother's son, he was sick for some months, then he seemed to get better, but a year or two later he started coughin' blood and him and his wife and kids all died. Lots of people died."

She measured the sweater against Liniculla's back, and Suzy poured her more of the rosehip tea. I put a stick of wood on the fire, but it was more to listen to it crackle than to heat the kitchen.

"That meant the next oldest boy was king and he did fine at the job. Had sense enough to ask for help if he needed it, which is more than can be said for some."

"When the Queen Mother died her oldest girl, my mother, became Queen Mother, only she never did have a son live long enough to become king, so her brother, my uncle, stood in as best he could. Things were real bad. People dyin' all over everywhere. One day there was no smoke at all from the village at Hecate, so the people from Kyuquot sent over a dugout to check, and they found the whole village dead. Every last one of'em, lyin' in their own mess and covered with sores. The Kyuquots stayed to try to burn the dead and before they'd finished, they were sick too. They headed home and took the sickness with them, and soon Kyuquot was under a thick smoke from the crematin' fires. People were burnin' up with fever so bad they'd run to the sea to cool off and the shock of the cold water on their burnin' bodies would just stop their hearts and they'd fall dead."

"My uncle did the best he could but the people were goin' crazy from havin' everyone they knew drop dead like that. My mother's sons all died young and by the time I was twelve my mother and my uncles were all dead, too."

"I was twelve and just finishin' my puberty trainin' and already I was Queen Mother. I had five uncles and two aunts and they were all married with big families, and my mother had four sons and five daughters but there I was gettin' ready for my big swim, and there was just me and my younger sister left. My sister, she had some spot scars on her face, but I only had some on my back and on one leg."

"They took me out in the dugout, like they'd always done, and I stood in the sea bird down, in all my best clothes and things, and they sang and they chanted, but they cried, too. The old woman, she stood near me, and she cried the whole way out, and it felt weird. I felt so proud and so happy that I'd finished my woman trainin', and I felt so sad and scared because I knew, even if nobody else did, that I wasn't ready to be no Queen Mother."

"There wasn't nothin' else to do though. I stripped off my stuff and I dove in the water and I started to swim back, chantin' the song in my head and strokin' in time to the music, and I just did what I'd been trained to do, even though I knew there'd be no mother and father waitin', proud and happy, and no aunts or grandmother. I cried, too. Salt tears and salt water, and the cold cuttin' into me, and once I almost just gave up and let the sea have me, but I knew my sister would have even more trouble than me, so I kept goin'. She hadn't been trained to be Queen Mother, and it wouldn't have been fair to her. And I stepped out on the beach, and I fell down, and old woman was cryin' and so was I, and then she put her cape around me and I just knew that's it, it's okay, nothin' else will be this bad."

"They had mission schools by then. Not government residential schools like came later, but church schools, and they started takin' the orphans and lookin' after them. They

103

came for my sister'n'me, but I ran off and hid and the people said I'd died. They believed that, since so many others had died already. And they only took my sister."

"I was supposed to be Queen Mother and I almost needed babysittin' myself. Stuff I should'a learned had died when the memorizers choked on diphtheria or died from whoopin' cough or rottin' sickness. The old women taught me what they knew, and old woman, she taught what she knew, and I stayed clear of the mission schools so it wasn't too bad. My sister, she was there until she turned fifteen. Then she'd learned all that they had to teach her, and she wanted to come home. But they said no, she hadda have someone to look after her. Never figured she could look after herself. So she had to stay two more years, workin' for them until she could arrange with a young man who wanted to go home, to marry her, and so the mission school was happy and let'em both leave. She had a little girl the next year and a boy two years later but she died havin' him so there was just me."

"I hadn't really thought much about gettin' married, I just didn't feel that it was what I wanted, and in the old days that might have been allowed, what with my sister havin' a boy to be king. But things had changed and it wasn't the old days and finally after listenin' a lot to the others, well, I figured I'd better get married and have some kids while there was still someone left alive to be a father, and I got married. Twice. First husband, he gave me two boys, then he went down with his fishboat and we never found his body. My oldest son by him would'a been king but they took him to residential school and he got the TB so they took him to hospital in Nanaimo, but he died there. I got married a second time just before he died, to your grandpa. We had a boy, then your momma. The second boy from my first husband, he went off to be a logger and got to drinkin' and took his car off the road and that was that."

"Your momma was six and I had another little boy and they took your momma off to residential school, and then the baby, he got sick and they said he should go to Nanaimo, too. So I talked to your grandpa and I told him I was tired of cryin' over kids that got took away and he agreed with me so from then on I drank the bug-weed tea and made sure I knew where the moon was all the time."

"Then your grandpa, he died. Big strong man, always laughin', always lovin'. He caught the measles from some kids and he died."

"Your momma ran away from residential school and haywired around Vancouver for a couple of years, and then, when she got out of jail, she came home and married up with your daddy. I never had much use for him or his family, myself, but your momma figured his summer socks were perfumed and he was real good to her. He'd brush her hair the way Suzy brushes yours, and he could always make her happy so I figured he couldn't be held to fault for his family all bein' driftwood and if your moma loved him it was good enough for me."

"If they'd'a had a son, he'd'a been king, but the fishboat motor blew up and they only had time to strap a life preserver on you and they were gone. Right out there in the bay."

"If she'd'a been raised to run and swim instead'a bein' in residential school, or if she'd'a trained for her puberty swim instead'a learnin' bible verses, she'd'a easy swum home to me."

"But she didn't." Granny stared at me so hard I got goosebumps all over, and shivered. "So you're all I got left in the whole world. I'm Queen Mother of nothin', and old woman to nobody and when I die, it'll all die with me."

"Unless," she grinned suddenly and pulled Liniculla onto her knee, "unless this one's ears are as big as her eyes."

THE WARRIOR WOMEN

*"We knew we couldn't stay out in the open
without bein' wiped out. It was a Time,
a time of Change, a time to wait and do nothin' until
we could see what needed done. So the women's
warrior society went secret, as secret as
the society of women . . ."*

THERE ARE DAYS on this island, especially in autumn
and wintertime, when the clouds sit blocking the sun,
and the rain falls until you feel as if the sound of it
hitting the roof is the only sound you've ever really known, a
sound driving you into yourself, hammering at your head until your knees begin to feel as if they're going to buckle. Just
when you're sure you can't stand another minute of water,
cloud, mist, and fog, the wind shifts, the sky clears, and
you'd almost think it was springtime.

We'd had nearly three weeks of rain and mud and were
making jokes about watching for an old man in a long robe,
going around collecting pairs of animals. Frankie Adams insisted he'd seen the old fellow, in gum boots, with an um-
brella, trying to talk my dog Lady into going in a big boat,
but Lady wasn't having any of it, so the old guy left. The
kids had been in and out of the houses so many times the
women were ready to lock the doors, and we all had floor-
itis from wiping up after muddy feet. Kids would come in

from playing in the puddles soaking wet and smeared with mud, and they'd just get into dry clothes and warm up a bit, and then they'd be outside again, leaving the laundry problem a bit bigger. We had clothes drying on lines and hooks, steaming up the windows and making us all feel even more hemmed in, and then the sun broke through and the rainbows started forming in the sky and we all went out to look at them.

"Just like the wings of dragonflies and butterflies," my granny smiled, nodding her approval. She was sitting on the porch, her fading eyesight feasting on the glory. We moved the washtubs into place and started the fussy old agitator machine on the porch, and got busy with the jeans and socks and heavy sweaters we hadn't been able to get clean washing by hand, and Liniculla helped me fill the rinse tub with cold water. We were barely into the first load when my granny started to talk, the soft flow of her voice counterpointed by the chug of the washing machine, the swish of the hot wash water against the stiff denim.

"The Fireweed Clan were the nurses," she told us. "Most of their women were disciples and the old woman would figure out what needed to be done for a sick person and mostly it was the Fireweed Clan would do the tendin' and carin'. When the epidemics hit, the Fireweed Clan was the worst affected and even though they knew it was almost sure death, they still looked after the sick. It was what they'd been trained to do, it was what they had always done, and even if the world was endin', that was no reason to stop their purpose in life. So many of them died there didn't seem to be enough left to continue as a clan, so they sang the songs, said the prayers, and retired it, and were accepted into the protection of other clans. Some are Bear Clan, now, some are Eagle Clan, some are Killer Whale, but we still know who was Fireweed because their families still got the right to wear the butterfly design, or the dragonfly, or the bee, or the hummingbird."

She flashed a special smile at Liniculla, who was helping me by lifting jeans from the rinse water and feeding them through the wringer. And Liniculla grinned happily because they both knew, now, that when Granny got finished embroidering the butterfly-in-four-colours onto the dance vest and gave it to Liniculla along with one of Granny's own special names, there would be something extra being told to all the people. The people would see Liniculla dancing in her vest, and hear Granny give her the name in a ceremony, and they would all know that even though she came from Suzy's body and not mine, even though Suzy was no blood kin to us and her blood and mine would never and could never mix to start a new life, we're both parents in Granny's eyes, and Liniculla was entitled to be considered Granny's great-grandaughter, inheriting from her as well as from Suzy's grandmother.

Liniculla has never known any of the women of the family of the man who planted the seed in Suzy's body. But she won't grow up without a full set of relatives because now she has all of Suzy's and all of mine, and she will know who she is and where she came from, so she'll know where she's supposed to be going. She knows she is of the retired Fireweed Clan, with a loving history of service and healing, and that the rainbows were in the sky to remind her nothing is ever destroyed completely, and the spirits of those who sacrificed themselves live on, coming together with the rain and sun to be a promise for us all. And when she dances in the vest with the butterfly-in-four-colours, all the people will know, too.

Granny had her hippy gear on, and we teased her about it, called her the oldest surviving flowerchild on the island and asked, did she want a plastic flower to push in her headband, and she just laughed at us and waved her fingers for us to keep feeding jeans through the wringer. She didn't always wear her hippy headband, just sometimes the mood would strike her and she'd put it on, tying her hair back with the black cord at the back. It looked like once it had been a hanky or a piece of cotton left over from a shirt or a dress, plain red cotton folded and knotted at the back. And through the knot, with both ends hanging down, and decorated with

some old trade beads, was this black ribbon or cord she used
to tie her hair out of the way.

We'd finished the wash and emptied the machine and had
all the jeans and heavy socks hanging on the line, flapping in
the stiff breeze from the sea, and some of the older women
came over to have tea with Granny. You could tell they'd
been washing, too, their hands were still puffy and wrinkled
from the water and they had their hair held in place by hippy headbands, too. There was a blue one with white dots you
knew had been a handkerchief, a sunshine yellow one, and my
stand-in granny, in case my own died and I needed help or
council, was wearing one that was orangey-red with a white
flower pattern.

Granny went into the house with the old women, Liniculla
went off to join her friends sailing little boats in the puddles,
and when Suzy and I finished hanging up the last of the
washing, we went inside. The old women were sitting around
the kitchen sipping tea, talking Nootka and laughing softly.
Suzy and I got cups and tea and sat listening, not par-
ticipating, and I was enjoying, as always, how my granny
was around these old women. She seemed freer, more relaxed,
she chose her words less carefully and laughed more often, as
if she felt safer with them than she was even with us.

"Not all fishers are skippers," my Granny said suddenly,
"but all skippers are fishers. In the time before the strangers
came, women were fighters same as men, and got the same
trainin'. Not all members of the women's warrior society were
members of the secret society of women, but all the members
of the secret society of women were members of the warrior
society. A woman warrior recognized the face of the enemy
and was prepared to do whatever was necessary to defeat it."

"Sometimes the women warriors would meet without the
men, to sit in a circle and talk women talk, and if a woman
had somethin' botherin' her, or puzzlin' her, or scarin' her, or
makin' her feel uneasy, she'd say what it was. She could take
all the time she needed to talk about it, but it was expected
she'd have put some of her own time into findin' the words

and not talk in circles, endlessly, takin' up everyone else's time."

"Then the other women in the circle who had maybe had somethin' the same happen in their lives would talk about it, and about what they'd done, or hadn't done, or should have done, and sometimes out of it would come an answer for the sister with problems. And even if not, sometimes it was enough to just have been heard and given love."

"It was expected that besides just talkin' about what was botherin' you, you'd *do* somethin' about it. Usually it's better to *do* almost anythin' than let things continue if they're botherin' you. But sometimes the best thing you can *do* is nothin'. Sometimes you have to wait for the right Time before you can do."

"A woman would come to the circle as often as she needed, but the circle wasn't there to encourage a woman to only talk about her problems. The first three times you came with the same story, the women would listen and try to help. But if you showed up a fourth time, and it was the same old tired thing, the others in the circle would just get up and move and re-form the circle somewhere else. They didn't say the problem wasn't important, they just said, by movin', that it was *your* problem and it was time you did somethin' about it, you'd taken up all the time in other people's lives as was goin' to be given to you, and it was time to stop talkin' and *do* somethin'.'"

"A woman might not know what was botherin' her. And it was fine to go to the circle, or even to ask to have one formed, and just sit with women, and listen and maybe get strength from smiles and cuddles and just bein' with women you knew loved you."

"A warrior woman had to be able to recognize the face of the enemy or she couldn't be a warrior woman. Anyone who just dithered around like a muddlehead and didn't *do* anythin' about her problems would have her warrior headband taken away and she'd have to start all over again, tryin' to qualify to get it back. Nobody with a drinkin' problem could be a warrior. There wasn't any drinkin' problem before the others came, but after they were here some people had their headbands removed when we all saw they couldn't stay sober. A person who couldn't control her bad moods or temper would lose her headband until she learned control because ragin' around at nothin' is wastin' energy needed against the enemy."

"When the foreigners came and the sickness started, the warriors got hit bad. The healers and Fireweed Clan women had been in the secret society and were the backbone of the women's warrior society, and they were gettin' the worst of it all. Soon there were hardly any women left in the warrior society, they'd died fightin' the Keestadores, or the sickness or age took them and there weren't many young women to take over from them. Since there were less and less young women in the warrior society, women from other clans were recruited into the secret society."

"We knew we couldn't stay out in the open without bein' wiped out. It was a Time, a time of Change, a time to wait and do nothin' until we could see what needed done. So the women's warrior society went secret, as secret as the society of women. Only the women in the warrior society knew who the others were. It was the only way to keep the secret safe."

"And for four generations it's been a secret. Only the most trusted of the sisterhood knew that some of us wore a band for more than to just hold our hair off our faces, or be a decoration. And sometimes women without the right would wear what we called Princess Headbands, but the warrior women always knew who was and who wasn't entitled to wear the mark. And it helped keep the secret. If people thought it was just fashion, like lipstick or brassieres or pointy-toed shoes, there was less chance of the truth bein' found out."

"And now it's a time of change again. Time to change. Women are recognizin' the enemy. Women are lookin' for truth. Speakin' to young women, tellin' them that rape isn't anythin' at all to do with love or even with lust, tellin' them it's just another way for some people to convince themselves they've got power, any old kind of power. Women are learnin' to use their bodies again, learnin' to defend themselves again, and speakin' the truth about alcohol and pills and body shame. Lookin' for truth, lookin' for support, and love, and a circle to join."

Granny took off her headband, held it in her old hands, smiling at it as if it was a living friend.

"The black ribbon is the Death Cord," she said proudly, "the sign of rememberin', rememberin' all the women who have died to protect the soft power. White women burned as witches, black women sold as slaves, yellow women crippled and sold like furniture, brown women raped, their bodies made sick with disease, murdered. The beads are special, each has its own magic, its own power, four on each end of the Death Cord because four is a full number, a true number. The Death Cord could be a shoe lace, and it would still be what it is, a mark of rememberin' all the sisters who came before us," and she put the old red cotton band back around her wrinkled brow, pulled it down and fastened the Death Cord around her bun again.

I looked at Suzy and thought of her own fight for life, the years of confusion, pain, and drunken parties, the time spent with foster parents, the years away from the village, going to the city schools. She got herself so buggered up in her head that Granny went to another society and got Suzy grabbed, and then came months of testing in the Big House.

Getting grabbed is scary, and it's probably the hardest thing a person will ever have to do in her life. Without warning, you're surrounded by figures with masks, so you don't know who anybody is. When you've grown up knowing the faces of all the people in the village, it's terrifying to all of a sudden not recognize anybody at all. And the dancers take you to the limits of what you can stand, they bring you face to face with every fear you ever had, and just before you go crazy they lead you back. With song and dance and ritual and magic, they lead you back from the very edge of total insanity so that nothing can ever really scare you again. You've seen the faces of your own worst fears, and lived through it, and come back, and from then you know your strength.

I knew my eyes were full, I could feel the tears on my face, and I knew the senior sisters could see, and share, what I was feeling. If ever anybody had to fight for survival, it was Suzy, and if ever anybody won a victory, it was her. It was after being grabbed that Suzy cleaned up her life, went to university, studied hard, and finally became a Para-medic. Bringing her baby Liniculla, she came home to work for her people, going to the small ports, and villages, healing the sick, and comforting the sad. She's been everything to me all my life, best-friend, secret-sharer, chosen sister, and crying shoulder, and even when she was lost, confused and frightened, her courage never failed.

We all had another cup of tea, and then the old women left, and we started supper, and then brought the washing in off the line and hung it up on the chords in the house, to finish drying. Suzy and Liniculla stayed for supper and we all went to bed with the jeans, socks and sweaters still hanging in the house, steaming up the windows and making the place smell like the outside breeze was trapped inside.

In the morning the rain was back, and I woke up feeling grumpy, listening to the sound of it on the roof. Suzy was still asleep, curled up like a kitten, and I could hear Granny and Liniculla in the kitchen, chattering together and starting breakfast. I didn't want to get up, but then Suzy opened her eyes and saw me glaring at the rain, and she put her foot against my back and pushed, so I was out of bed whether I wanted to be or not.

"Somethin' came," Granny motioned with her head, handing us each a cup of coffee. Just in front of the door were two brown paper bags, like the ones the kids take their lunch in to school. One of the bags had my name printed on it in pencil, the other had Suzy's name. It looked as if some time during the night someone had just opened the front door, reached in, put the bags on the floor and left again.

I opened the bag with my name on it and brought out a folded red cotton hanky, knotted at the back, with a black shoe lace dangling from the knot. I held it, unable to find words, staring stupidly.

"We're recruitin' again," Granny said contentedly, laying bacon slices in the black cast iron frying pan. "Invitin' women who recognize the face of the enemy and are willin' to *do* somethin' about it to join us. You don't have to," she added quietly, "if you don't feel ready to shoulder the load, that's your choice."

Suzy left the house and came back with the eagle feather her grandmother had given her before she died, and she sat sewing while the bacon and eggs cooked and her first cup of coffee grew cold. She replaced the shoe lace with a length of black ribbon, and passed it through the knot of her blue headband. I beaded my shoe lace with big blue trading beads and then, feeling scared and proud and a lot of other things, I handed the headband to Granny, while Liniculla watched enviously.

"Granny?" was all I said, but she knew what I wanted. She waited while I turned so my back was to her, and I scrunched down, because she's lots shorter than I am, and then my granny put my headband in place and fastened the Death Cord around my braid, and gave me a little pat on the head.

"That's it," she said, and I don't think I ever heard her sound more content.

Suzy looked as if she was feeling all the things I was feeling, and she kind of gulped, then handed her headband to Granny. She sat down quickly, blinking fast, and Liniculla and I grinned at each other as Granny's wrinkled old hands fussed, making sure Suzy's warrior woman band was Just So.

"Looks good," Granny approved.

"Feels good," Suzy and I said at the same time. And then we were all laughing and hugging each other and feeling so good even the endless rain couldn't take the shine off the day.

THE FACE OF OLD WOMAN

*"There's a power other than the power
we live with every day. It's the power that
taught levitation. It's the power that lets us
leave our bodies and fly like songbirds . . ."*

THE RAIN WAS bashing against the windows, the deep black night pressed close against the side of the house, like a hungry bear wanting to be allowed in to warm itself by swallowing the lamplight. The kettle was steaming on the big black woodburning stove and the sound of the clic-clic-clic of Granny's knitting needles snapped through the music coming from the radio. Suzy was making her regular monthly tour of all the outports and villages, and she'd taken Liniculla with her to show her just what it was when mommy packed her things and went away for a week to do Community Health Care Work, and to show her some of the places she went to when the mickeymouse radio started squacking in the middle of the night and Suzy started running with her bags for the speedboat Big Bill already had gassed up and waiting.

I was sitting at the table with my red covered 250-page spiral notebook, trying to write down the stories Granny had

115

given me permission to put on paper for the first time, and I was chewing the plastic cap of my pen, staring holes in the wall, not getting much down on paper at all.

"You look like someone who's havin' trouble," Granny invited.

I could have let it pass by making a joke about trying to find English words for Nootka ideas, and even though she would have known I was evading, Granny would have accepted that. She was only inviting confidence, not demanding it. But I had been waiting for an invitation for days, and was glad to get it aired.

"I'm having trouble," I admitted.

"Want to tell me?"

She kept right on knitting, but her old eyes locked with mine, and I knew she already had a good idea of what I was chewing at myself about, and had known for almost as long as I'd been chewing.

"It's the stories." I put the pen down, and talked to the third eye, the one few people use any more, the one you can't see but that exists, just up above the nose. "All these years all this has been kept secret. Anybody got a whiff of it and asked, we'd just smile and say, 'Secret Society of Women? Must be a real big secret, I never heard of it.' Being taught since I was little not to tell certain stuff to people, to give the anthropologists and ethnologists and linguists and such only the stuff they wanted to hear, giving them nothing at all when they came poking around asking questions. And now, all of a sudden, it's okay to put it on paper. Maybe even write a book and let other people know."

"Other women," Granny corrected. "It was up to us to keep the secrets because the longrobes wanted to destroy the truth. Well, we kept it. Like a little bonfire, feedin' our lives like bits of wood, one or two at a time, keepin' it goin'. But it's not just ours."

Usually it's me gets up and gets the cups and the sugar and makes the tea. Tonight it was Granny, and I just sat and watched her, bustling around the kitchen, the short, pudgy, wrinkle-faced old woman who'd spent her whole life feeding a bonfire and spent most of my life looking after me. Lots of people would probably think she's kind of homely. She's as wrinkled as a dried apple, and years of walking have made the veins in her legs swell and arthritis is getting into her joints so she walks with a bit of a limp, rolling, like a fisherman first back from fishing, not yet used to the ground after days on a rolling deck. You look at her and you know it's been a long, hard life full of pain and tears. And I don't think I've ever known anybody as beautiful.

She gave me my cup of tea and went back to her chair by the stove, and I stared at the steam coming from the cup and tried to find some answers, and of course there weren't any.

"When the four families went off after the flood," she was talking but not looking at me, "they took knowledge with them, and I don't know what happened or what went wrong. I don't even know what all places they went to. But somethin' happened, because the knowledge got buggered. There's maybe bits of it all over, scattered bits, but most of it's lost. Only here, where it started, did the women manage to save most of it. But we didn't save all of it. When the sickness came, too many of us died, and what we've got is incomplete."

She was slipping in and out of English and Nootka now, sipping her tea, watching shadows in the room only she could see, calling on the power to help her.

"This isn't stuff just for Nootka, or just for Indian, or just for Indian women, or just for the few of us in the society. This stuff is for women. Black women, from the grandchildren of Copper Woman who became the parents of the black people. Yellow women, they got the same grandparents as us when you go back far enough. White women, they come from the belly of Old Woman, too. What did we save it for if we don't share? Less of us in the society every year. Old ones die and the young ones got educated by the invader, and they don't know, and we can't trust'em enough to teach'em all. A secret can die, sometimes. And a secret can kill, sometimes. But a book, maybe some women will read it and they'll Know."

"Granny," I could hear the shaking in my voice, "if this gets put in a book and we find someone to print it . . . you know what's going to happen?"

"Sure," she grinned, "every expert in every university is gonna have a shitfit! Gonna be pointin' to all the books written by all the men and gonna say it's all a pack'a'lies. Gonna scream that the books the men wrote tell the truth and this one's just make-believe."

"Granny, look what happened when we tried to tell them at the university that we'd travelled by dugout to both Hawaiian islands before Cook got there."

"Yeah," she giggled, "they wanted to know what year it was, and when we couldn't tell'em on their calendar they said we hadn't been there. So what? This stuff isn't for the men anyway. It isn't for the ones who cuddle the books full of lies. This stuff is for the women." She pierced me with her argylite eyes. "You told me there wasn't nothin' in university for you! You told me they talked a language nobody could understand anyway! You told me it made you sick to hear all the stuff they said that made you feel like they had no respect for women, or for Indians, and there you were both, and so you wouldn't go."

"Well, it's true," I defended.

"Good," she settled back in her chair. "Let'em think it's all bullshit. The women who can't find no peace in what the men's universities teach will maybe find peace in this stuff."

"Granny, I'm scared," I confessed.

"Yeah. I know you are. I just don't understand why you are. So I'm askin'."

"They'll go to the politicians first. They'll go to the men and ask them if this is true. And most of the Indian men in politics don't know about the Secret Society."

"Lots of'em do know," Granny corrected, "they just been brought up that it's the women's business, and it's secret, and they keep it secret."

"Well, what if they say it's bullshit."

"So what if they do? Their grandmothers told'em not to tell

anyone. Good men do what their grandmothers tell'em. Don't matter what the men say, long as *we* know."

"Granny, everything we ever had has been stolen from us. What if . . ." I just couldn't finish.

"Can't steal what's been offered with love," she looked at me as if she was disappointed that, after all those years of trying to teach me, I was still a few bricks short a full load. "There's gonna be women jump up and start tryin' to make a religion out of it and tryin' to sound like experts and tryin' to feel big and look clever in front of other women. And they'll get tired after a while, and give up, but the truth will still be there for the ones who keep lookin' for it. You worry too much, Ki-Ki."

"You said it yourself. Even our own young women. We can't trust them all because of how they've been educated."

"Can't trust'em to keep it secret," she agreed, "but if it ain't secret no more, there's no reason not to trust'em. They're women. Some of'em will be jealous that they weren't told, and they'll holler that it's lies, but we got to learn to hate what they're doin' and still love them. It's not their fault, Ki-Ki. They been educated to be controlled by men. But they're women. We gotta trust somethin'."

She looked at me with tears in her eyes, "I'm tired, Ki-Ki. Deep inside me, in a place I never been tired before, I'm tired. I'm the old woman and there aren't enough sisters in the society to give me back the strength I need when I feel tired like this. I gotta have faith in myself. I gotta have faith in Old Woman. I gotta have faith in you and the thing you want to do. There's gotta be a reason that you been scratchin' stuff on paper since you was eleven years old. There's gotta be a reason that your writin' happened at a time when women everywhere was standin' up and sayin' they want to know woman's truth, no more longrobe bullshit."

"Sometimes," she remembered her cup of tea and took a sip, and her voice found strength, "sometimes you just gotta trust that your secret's been kept long enough."

It felt good to me, and I was just about ready to make another attempt to get words on paper. Granny poured more tea and put another stick in the fire and when she turned, she wasn't my Granny any more. Her face was hard-edged, her mouth looked like the top of a drawstring bag that's been pulled shut, all puckered and lined, and thousands of years old. I stared into the face of Old Woman, and felt the chair under me start to melt away, the table disappear, until there was just Old Woman talking with my Granny's voice, but Granny's voice altered, just Old Woman and me, alone in a place that wasn't the kitchen of the house I live in.

"There's more," the voice filled my head "there's a power other than the power we live with every day. It's the power that taught levitation. It's the power that lets us leave our bodies and fly like spiritbirds, and it's the power that allows Old Woman to be fog, or mist, or ride the wind, or speak through the old woman."

"This power has been around for a long long time, in more worlds than this one, on more earths than this one. And just as the opposite of fire is water, the opposite of hot is cold, the opposite of hard is soft, the opposite of man is woman, there's an opposite to the power that is good. And it's a power that is evil. And not everyone knows the difference."

"Our island sisters died of sickness, alcohol, confusion, and fear, to defend the soft power. Other sisters in other places died of torture, by burning, by drowning, by the cross-hilt sword, in defence of the soft power. All over this earth, for as long as there's been people, women have died to protect the secrets. If the enemy knows which of us know the face of evil, they attack. 'Thou shalt not suffer a witch to live', and women die because the cold, hard power doesn't want women to learn we weren't made to be used and controlled."

"Women are bringing the pieces of the truth together. Women are believing again that we have a right to be whole. Scattered pieces from the black sisters, from the yellow sisters, from the white sisters, are coming together, trying to form a whole, and it can't form without the pieces we have saved and cherished. Without the truth we have protected, women won't have the weapons of defence they need. If we hold our secret to ourselves any longer, we help the evil ones destroy the Womanspirit."

"We must reach out to our sisters, all of our sisters, and ask them to share their truth with us, offer to share our truth with them. And we can only trust that this gift, from woman to woman, be treated with love and respect, in a way opposite from the way the evil treated the other things this island had. Rivers are filthy that used to be clean. Mountains are naked that used to be covered with trees. The ocean is fighting for her life and there are no fish where there used to be millions, and this is the work of the cold evil. The last treasure we have, the secrets of the matriarchy, can be shared and honoured by women, and be proof there is another way, a better way, and some of us remember it."

"There is more than one road to the afterlife, there is more than one way to love, there is more than one way to find the other half of self in another person, there is more than one way to fight the enemy."

And then I was back at the kitchen table, and Granny was sitting in her rocking chair, staring at the floor, looking so old, and so tired I knew, suddenly and sadly, that Time for her was coming full. I got up, moved to the stove, and added wood to the almost extinguished coals. I went to Granny and I held her, and she knew I was there, even though she didn't move or speak, and I went away from her to allow her time to come back into her own body, the body so recently occupied by Old Woman. When the kettle was boiling, I made tea for my Granny, and she smiled, and I kissed her cheek, and then sat down at my book to write.

I didn't hear Granny get up, I didn't see her refill my cup of tea, I didn't hear her slow footsteps as she headed off to her bed. I picked up my pen, stared at it for a few minutes, then I felt my face go hard, my mouth pucker, my body go cold, and when I came back to this world, the stove was out, I was chilled and stiff, my tea was cold, and my pages covered with what might be a poem, or maybe several poems, or maybe a song, or maybe several songs, or maybe all of that. And I knew then, and know now, that what we have protected on this island is not complete, the knowledge is scattered, and if we offer all women what we know, the scattered pieces can start to re-form, and those who need to find courage, peace, truth and love will learn that these things are inside all of us, and can be supported by the truth of women.

I am the sea

I am the mountains

I am the light

I am eternal

This confusion is fog
There is light beyond
I sense it and feel its warmth

I move toward it
but not headlong
I fear to stumble,
to fall with pain,

There are women everywhere with fragments
when we learn to come together we are whole
when we learn to recognize the enemy
we will come to recognize what we need to know
to learn how to come together

I know the many smiling faces of my enemy
I know the pretense that is the weapon used.
I have been the enemy
and learn to know myself well.

The ones who talk only from the throat
see only with two eyes
hear only with ears
but pretend to do more
are the enemy

THE FACE OF OLD WOMAN

I walk amidst shards
and fear laceration
I must dare to bleed
I must dare to cut myself
To amputate
the festering pain

I will learn to mix
medicine bags for those with faith
I will learn to chant the power chant
I will learn to mix
medicine bags for those with faith
I will learn to chant the power chant
and play the healing drum
I will not fear moss voices
        water songs
        small furry things with sharp teeth
        or my own hesitancy

I am falling
I am falling

        past star
        past time
        through space
        and my own fragments

oh sisters the pain

I am scattered
I am scattered

        gather fragments
        weave and mend
        scattered fragments
        weave and mend

In golden light
I recognize the enemy faces

fear of our bodies
fear of our visions
fear of our healing
fear of our love
fear of sisterkind
fear of brotherkind
fear of fear

> *love is healing*
> *healing is love*

There are Women everywhere with fragments
> *gather fragments*
> *weave and mend*
When we learn to come together we are whole
When we learn to recognize the enemy
we will know what we need to know
to learn how to come together
to learn how to weave and mend

Old Woman is watching
Watching over you
> *in the darkness of the storm*
> *she is watching*
> *watching over you*

> *weave and mend*
> *weave and mend*

Old Woman is watching
> *watching over you*
with her bones become a loom
> *she is weaving*
> *watching over us*
> *weave and mend*
> *golden circle*
> *weave and mend*
> *sacred sisters*
> *weave and mend*

THE FACE OF OLD WOMAN

I have been searching
lost
alone
I have been searching
for so many years

I have been searching
Old Woman

and I find her
in
mySelf

Also of interest:

Paula Gunn Allen, editor
Spider Woman's Granddaughters
Traditional Tales and Contemporary Writing
by Native American Women

'**Every story in the book, which covers nearly a
century of tradition, is interesting, written with
intelligent passion; several are real treasures . . .
Despite its richness, the book may be read right
through without surfeit. But one will want also to
dwell on individual pieces, as one's gaze returns to
the bluest turquoises in a fine bracelet . . .**'
Ursula K Le Guin, *New York Times Book Review*

'**Compelling**' *Publishers Weekly*

'**Alive and potent with literary magic**'
Philadelphia Inquirer

According to Cherokee legend, Grandmother Spider
brought the light of intelligence and experience to the
people. *Spider Woman's Granddaughters* is a marvellous
collection of traditional tales, biographical writings and
contemporary stories by her spiritual and literary
granddaughters. Although many speak of individual and
cultural loss, of pain and poverty, they offer a joyful vision of
pride in personal and tribal identity, and demonstrate the
richness and range of Native American writing.

Fiction   £6.95
ISBN: 0 7043 4238 3

Patricia Grace
Potiki

A beautifully told story by one of New Zealand's finest writers.

'And from this place of now, behind, and in and beyond the tree, from where I have eversight, I watch the people. The people work and watch and wait. They pace the tides and turn the earth. They stand, listening on the shores.'

A small Maori coastal community whose land and way of life are threatened by property developers is at the heart of this rich and vivid tale. The people draw on the strength of their own relationships, their respect for each other as well as for the place they inhabit.

Granny McDonald – who is the community's consistent source of calm and reason.

Mary – who finds herself pregnant as a young girl.

Tokowaru-i-te-Marama – the prophet child, who can see with sinister accuracy the advent of a new but horrifying era.

Fiction   £3.95
ISBN: 0 7043 4081 X